The Gathering

Arje Shaw

A SAMUEL FRENCH ACTING EDITION

SAMUEL FRENCH

FOUNDED 1830

SAMUELFRENCH.COM
SAMUELFRENCH-LONDON.CO.UK

FOR PRODUCTION ENQUIRIES

UNITED STATES AND CANADA
Info@SamuelFrench.com
1-866-598-8449

UNITED KINGDOM AND EUROPE
Plays@SamuelFrench-London.co.uk
020-7255-4302

Each title is subject to availability from Samuel French, depending upon country of performance. Please be aware that *THE GATHERING* may not be licensed by Samuel French in your territory. Professional and amateur producers should contact the nearest Samuel French office or licensing partner to verify availability.

THE GATHERING was first produced at Playhouse 91 as a co-production of Diaspora Productions and The Jewish Repertory Theater in New York City on May 29, 1999. The performance was directed by Rebecca Taylor with sets by Robert Joel Schwartz, costumes by Susan L. Soetaert, lighting by Scott Clyve, music by Andy Stein, and sound by Jeremy Posner. The Production Stage Manager was D. C. Rosenberg. The cast was as follows:

GABE	Theodore Bikel
MICHAEL	Jesse Eisenberg
STUART	Robert Fass
DIANE	Susan Hasho
EGON	Peter Hermann

THE GATHERING opened on Broadway at the Cort Theater in New York City on April 24, 2001. The performance was directed by Rebecca Taylor with sets by set designer, costumes by Susan Soetaert, lighting by Scott Clyve, sound by T. Richard Fitzgerald, sound effects by Jeremy Posner, and music by Andy Stein. The Production Stage Manager was Dom Ruggiero. The cast was as follows:

GABE	Hal Linden
MICHAEL	Max Dworin
STUART	Sam Guncler
DIANE	Deirdre Lovejoy
EGON	Coleman Zeigen

CHARACTERS

GABE (ZAYDEE) – Michael's Grandfather
MICHAEL (BOYTSCHICK) – Grandson
STUART – Michael's Father
DIANE – Michael's Mother
EGON – Young German Security Guard

SETTING

A New York City apartment in 1985, and the German cemetery, Bitberg.

TIME

1980s

Dedicated to Bina, Gabe, and Miriam

ACT ONE

Scene One

(April 11, 1985. Friday afternoon, 4:00 p.m., N.Y.C.
GABE, *called "Zaydee," is a sculptor who works out of his studio apartment cluttered with books, newspapers, sculpted busts of biblical and political figures, and one bust in progress of Muhammad Ali next to a boxing poster as a frame of reference. A chess board sits on a coffee table. Lights come up on* **GABE** *chiseling the Ali bust, listening to the radio news report and talking back to the radio.)*

RADIO. (*voiceover*) And on the local front, Mayor Koch is heading to Albany to demand financial support for a clean up campaign to remove graffiti from the subway, stating that New Yorkers deserve safe, clean, subway cars and stations. Koch is furious at the State for holding up the funding of the project which is six months delayed.

GABE. So what else is new?

(radio jingle)

RADIO. (*voiceover*) You're listening to News Watch New York. 10-10 Wins on your dial. News, weather, and traffic, every hour on the hour, twenty-four hours a day. You give us twenty-two minutes, we give you the world! *(radio jingle)* Sunny but cold in the Big Apple on gridlock Friday, April 11, 1985. The White House announced that President Reagan has been invited by West German Chancellor, Helmut Kohl, to keynote the European Economic Conference in Bonn, Germany. This visit will mark the 40th anniversary-

GABE. Forty years,

RADIO. (*voiceover*) Of peaceful co-existence between the United States and Germany.

GABE. Peace,

RADIO. (*voiceover*) Since the end of the Second World War.

GABE. Bitter enemies become best friends!

RADIO. (*voiceover*) President and Mrs. Reagan will be guests of honor at a State-sponsored Gala hosted by Chancellor Helmet Kohl.

GABE. What mother names her child "Helmut?" He must have been a cute baby!

RADIO. (*voiceover*) With this visit, President Reagan aligns himself with Chancellor Kohl, who is fighting for his political life in a heated re-election campaign, against anti-American extremists, who vow to remove U.S. military troops and missiles. Kohl has pledged full support of the NATO Alliance stating Germany's friendship with the United States is unshakeable. He said, "The past is the past."

GABE. Easy for him to say! I throw a helmet right at his head! Besterd! (*switching dial*) Who can listen to this chazerai crap? I need a vacation from the news! (*stops at a Yiddish station playing "Rummenia"*) Aaah! that's better!

(*singing and chiseling in rhythm with the upbeat "Rummenia"*)

Hi d'ge d'ge d'ge dom!
Hi d'ge d'ge d'ge dom!
Hi d'ge d'ge d'ge-

(*accidentally nicks the bust*)

Ay-yay-yay! What did I do?! What did I do?! Muhammad Ali fights a hundred fights not a mark on his face, and I stupid schmuck put a dent in his head! Ach, I'm such a big shot! The giants Michelangelo, Lipchitz, Roden, Epstein, they work in marble, alabaster, clay, bronze, and I, artist schmuck that I am, pick granite, the hardest stone. ACH! I'm so disgusted mit myself... Let me see what I can do here to repair the damage, file down, fill in, cover up, camouflage, *(speaking to the Ali bust)*... Don't worry bubbele, Poppa Gabe will fix you right up! No one will know a thing! It will be our secret, *(Buzzer sounds.)* AHA! That's my Boytschick! You'll excuse me my good friend, I don't care if you are The Champion of the World, my grandson comes first! Family before Art! *(presses the intercom) (beat)* I feel a draft. *(to Ali bust)* You feel a draft? Never enough heat in this farkakte apartment. But it's controlled rent. The landlord controls the rent. *(bangs his foot on the floor)* Turn up the heat you cheap bestard! Momser goes to Florida and I freeze my toches in New York! But at least there's life here! My Boytschick's here, my grandson, Michael!

*(**MICHAEL** bursts through the door, tosses his backpack full of books aside.)*

MICHAEL. FREE AT LAST! FREE AT LAST! THANK GOD ALMIGHTY, I'M FREE AT LAST!

GABE. SHALOM ALAYCHEM MARTIN LUTHER KING!

MICHAEL. *(They embrace.)* This is the best day, Zaydee!

GABE. Why, Boytschick, are the teachers on strike again?

MICHAEL. It's Easter break! No school for two whole weeks!

GABE. And what about Hebrew school?

MICHAEL. Closed!

GABE. A Hebrew school closed for Easter?

MICHAEL. It's a good year, Zaydee, Passover and Easter come out at the same time.

GABE. In the first place, Passover ended a week ago. And in the second place, we celebrate Passover to remember our history, not to forget it.

MICHAEL. I thought we celebrate Passover for the matzo balls and macaroons.

GABE. You're such a wise guy? Answer me this! Who took the Jews out of Egypt?

MICHAEL. Moses.

GABE. His brother?

MICHAEL. Aaron!

GABE. His sister?

MICHAEL. Miriam!

GABE. His mother?

MICHAEL. Yocheved!

GABE. His father?

MICHAEL. Seymore!

GABE. Seymore?!

MICHAEL. Amram.

GABE. Amram! You win the prize! Catch! *(flips him a Hershey kiss)*

MICHAEL. A Hershey kiss! Umm, I love chocolate!

GABE. You're a real chocolodnik!

MICHAEL. Chocoholic!

GABE. No, Chocolodnik! That's what we called the American soldiers, when they liberated us from the camps, they gave us Hershey bars. Oy, was that Hershey good! We licked our fingers to the bone, which wasn't too far from the truth, because we were starving to death! Chocolate eating skeletons! Even, Hitler would have been scared looking at us! Oy, I got so sick, Boytschick, I ate too many chocolates, did I ever tell you the time I –

MICHAEL. How's the Ali coming? *(walks to the bust)*

GABE. Take a look. It's my best work! Perfect, smooth. Not a scratch!

MICHAEL. *(points to the nick)* Zaydee! There's a hole in Ali's head!

GABE. *(smacks his hand away)* It's nothing! I gave him some room to breathe.

MICHAEL. Ali's looking really great.

GABE. I love this man!

MICHAEL. It shows Zaydee, in his face, his eyes.

GABE. What a champion. What courage. Ali gave up the best five years of his life for a cause he believed in. He fought in the ring but refused to fight in Viet Nam! A conscious objector!

MICHAEL. Conscientious.

GABE. That too! He lifted his people without landing a single blow. Muhammed Ali walked the walk! Talked the talk! And took no crap! You hear, Boytschick, you hear?

MICHAEL. I hear, I hear, *(He's heard it all before.)*

GABE. When you have a Right! You have a Right!

MICHAEL. Right.

GABE. And, Boy, did have a Right!

MICHAEL. Right.

GABE. **POW!!**

MICHAEL. *(meekly)* Pow.

GABE. I saw all his fights Boytschick.

MICHAEL. I know Zaydee,

GABE. All of them.

MICHAEL. I know.

GABE. Every one!

MICHAEL. I know.

GABE. Didn't miss a one!

MICHAEL. Not one.

GABE. The "Thriller in Manila"! The "Rumble in the Jungle"!

MICHAEL. *(covers his ears)* Oh God!

GABE. The Foreman!

MICHAEL. Yes.

GABE. The Norton!

MICHAEL. Yes.

GABE. The Frazier!

MICHAEL. I know.

GABE. The Sphinx!

MICHAEL. Yes!

GABE. The Sonny Liston!

MICHAEL. Yes! I know!

GABE. You know?

MICHAEL. I know, I know, Zaydee! Believe me, I know! You're such a nudnik!

GABE. So what made Ali great?

MICHAEL. He had a big mouth.

GABE. What else?

MICHAEL. A big punch.

GABE. Vos noch?

MICHAEL. He was strong.

GABE. And

MICHAEL. Brave.

GABE. And

MICHAEL. Ali believed in himself!

GABE. AAH! Now you're talking!

MICHAEL. Muhammad spoke his heart!

GABE. Tell it like it is!

MICHAEL. He stood up to the world!

GABE. A beautiful black man!

MICHAEL. Tall and proud.

GABE. Tall and proud.

MICHAEL. Strong and brave.

GABE. Strong and brave.

MICHAEL/GABE. A TZADIK!!

> (*They go into a synchronized shadow-box rap dance routine.*)

Float like a butterfly,

Sting like a bee

I don't give a damn

What you say about me.

I'm gonna say what I think

N' do what I say.

If you don't like it,
Just get out of my way!
Oy – och n'vay
Oy – och n'vay
If you don't like it,
Just stay out of my way!

MICHAEL. OY – OCH N'VAY

GABE. OY – OCH N'VAY

MICHAEL/GABE. IF YOU DON'T LIKE IT,
SAY OCH N'VAY! YEAH !

(fist in the air, then high five slap)

GABE. Now that's the kind of responsive reading we should do for your Bar Mitzvah!

MICHAEL. I don't think the Rabbi would like it.

GABE. But the Congregation sure would! *(beat)* Ready for a game of chess?

MICHAEL. I'm always ready, but if you want to work on the Ali, instead –

GABE. What, and break my winning streak?

MICHAEL. Your winning streak is over!

GABE. Oooh such arrogance. I love it! Who taught you such arrogance?

MICHAEL. You did.

GABE. That's what I want to hear! Set up the board Boytschick while I heat us up some chicken soup. We need strength for this match!

MICHAEL. *(setting up the board)* You made chicken soup?

GABE. From fresh chickens! Just like your Bobbe used to make!

MICHAEL. You can't cook!

GABE. Hey! Just because I chisel stone, doesn't mean I have stone fingers.

MICHAEL. *(confusing aroma)* I don't know Zaydee, it doesn't smell like chicken soup.

GABE. Of course it's chicken soup. I even put in some kreplach. *(depositing container of wonton soup into a pot)*

MICHAEL. Ooh Kreplach?! I love Kreplach! *(runs over, lifts the lid on the pot)* ZAYDEE!! THESE ARE WONTONS!!

GABE. Wontons, kreplach, what's the difference! As long as it tastes good!

MICHAEL. But you're Kosher!

GABE. I'm Kosher, I'm Kosher, but my next door neighbor's Korean. What should I do, insult Mrs. Moon Kim Sang? It's nice she thinks of me.

MICHAEL. *(beat)* You miss Bubbee Molly?

GABE. Married forty years, I shouldn't miss her?

MICHAEL. I miss her too... Bubbee made the best kreplach. *(beat)* Zaydee, what happens to people when they die?

GABE. *(brings over two soup bowls and they eat)* A piece of you dies with them, Boytschick. It's not like kreplach, that you can replace with wontons.

MICHAEL. I'm serious Zaydee. Do you believe when people die, they die forever?

GABE. If you let them.

MICHAEL. What do you mean?

GABE. If you forget them, if you don't cherish their memories, then they die.

MICHAEL. You think they can come back?

GABE. No. Once you're dead! You're dead! That's it! Kaput!

MICHAEL. How can you be so sure?

GABE. Many things I'm not sure. This I'm sure.

MICHAEL. On TV, a man said he came back.

GABE. From where, the drug store?

MICHAEL. The other side Zaydee. He said it was very peaceful.

GABE. So why didn't he stay there?

MICHAEL. You don't think it's peaceful on the other side?

GABE. Depends who you bump into.

MICHAEL. Did you see many people die?

GABE. Too many…

MICHAEL. You have memories?

GABE. Too many…

MICHAEL. You should try to forget Zaydee.

GABE. I try, I try, but they keep reminding me! 40 years since the war! 50 years since Kristallnacht! It's Holocaust season in America! Enough already! It's bad enough I lived through it. You don't have to bring up a tragedy to remind you, you're part of one.

MICHAEL. I don't know what I would have done if the Nazi's came for me.

GABE. What could you do?

MICHAEL. Run away?

GABE. To where?

MICHAEL. Anywhere, get some help.

GABE. Who helps the Jew? No one.

MICHAEL. Zaydee, sometimes I think that if the Holocaust didn't happen, then I wouldn't be here, that if the Holocaust-

GABE. *(cuts in)* Enough with the Holocaust! Let the games begin! *(Timing bell is tapped.* GABE *suddenly jumps up.)* OY! Why didn't you remind me?!

MICHAEL. What, you left a brisket in the oven?

GABE. Shah! Don't be a wise guy. Your Haftarah!

MICHAEL. Oh come on, not now, we're playing chess!

GABE. *(takes the prayer book)* Boytschick, your Bar Mitzvah's in two weeks! You must practice!

MICHAEL. I've been practicing for two years, Zaydee! it's a five-minute G'Shichte!

GABE. Do it!

MICHAEL. Why do I have to do it if I know it?

GABE. Because I promised your parents.

MICHAEL. They promise me things all the time! Dad promised to come to my class!

GABE. Boytschick, your father's not a plumber, he's a speechwriter in the White House.

MICHAEL. Big deal!

GABE. It is a big deal! How many boys your age can say their Poppa writes propaganda for the President! You should be kvelling!

MICHAEL. Yeah, I'm kvelling.

GABE. Boytschick, your Poppa's in the White House. A Jew in the White House! My son! Your father!

MICHAEL. He doesn't have time for me, Zaydee!

GABE. But, that's what Zaydees are for! You must understand Boytschick, your Poppa's a busy man. A big shot! Who knows, he could become another Henry Kissinger!

MICHAEL. Who's Henry Kissinger?

GABE. Oh! Dr. Henry Kissinger! A brilliant Jewish diplomat, with a heavy, annoying German accent. As soon as he'd open his mouth, the hair on my neck would stand up. But what he had to say was brilliant!

MICHAEL. Dad's not brilliant. He's just a speechwriter.

GABE. Just a speechwriter? Do you read his books?

MICHAEL. They're boring.

GABE. It's history!

MICHAEL. History's boring.

GABE. Not if you live through it. Do your Haftarah!

MICHAEL. But I did it for you last week.

GABE. Last week was a week ago. You have no idea what you can forget in a week!

MICHAEL. That's you!

GABE. *(pulls the bowl away)* No Haftarah! No soup!

MICHAEL. But, I'm hungry!

GABE. You don't study, you don't eat!

MICHAEL. But, Zaydee, even you say the whole Bar Mitzvah's a bunch of baloney.

GABE. I never said that.

MICHAEL. Yes you did! You said it's a show. The Bar Mitzvah's a show. That's what you say!

GABE. It is a show. But the idea isn't.

MICHAEL. What's the idea? To wear a stupid suit you hate! Strangers spray food all over my face, pinch my cheeks, stuff envelopes in my pockets, asking me what it feels like to be a man!

GABE. Boytchick, don't be so cynical. Not yet. You have time. The idea, the idea of a Bar Mitzvah is to celebrate the beginning of becoming a man.

MICHAEL. Zaydee, you don't become a man because Sisterhood gives you a Kiddush cup or the Men's Club gives you Shabbes candle sticks!

GABE. It's the other way around, Sisterhood gives you candlesticks, and the Men's Club-

MICHAEL. *(cuts him off)* Who cares! What I'm trying to say is that you don't become a man when you get something. It's when you do something. Something that's important. Something that's hard to do…like the Indians.

GABE. Indians?

MICHAEL. You know, Zaydee! The Indians, the American Indians?! When it was time for boys to become men, boys my age, would go out into the wilderness all alone, live in the cold, in the night, in the woods, among the wild animals! Now that was a Bar Mitzvah!

GABE. Boytschick, surviving a Bar Mitzvah in a catering hall, is a wilderness all by itself! A JEWISH WILDERNESS! Plenty of Vilda Chayes, wild animals to watch out for, especially around the dessert table.

MICHAEL. Zaydee, I'm serious. Don't you think you should do something important to become a man? Something that really means something to prove that you deserve it?

GABE. Of course.

MICHAEL. I've never done that, Zaydee. What have I done that's important? I go to school, do my homework, and that's my life!

GABE. Boytschick your time will come.

MICHAEL. When Zaydee? When will I become a man? When will everyone stop treating me like a kid! *(jumping up and down, frustrated)* I want to do something! I want to do something! I want to do something important!

GABE. Practice your Haftarah.

MICHAEL. No!

GABE. Boy-tschick?

MICHAEL. I'll make you an offer!

GABE. No offers! What is it?

MICHAEL. We play. You win, I do Haftarah! I win, I'll see you at the Bar Mitzvah!

GABE. *(beat)* Move Pisher!

MICHAEL. *(They sit.)* My pleasure! *(Three quick moves followed by tap on bell after each move.)* *(fourth move)* Knight to rook three! *(Game of chess escalates to a game of will.)*

GABE. Knight to Bishop three.

MICHAEL. King's Pawn!

GABE. King's pawn? Hah! *(laughs)* I'm gonna whup your toches! *(moves)*

MICHAEL. Let your fingers do the talking! *(moves)*

GABE. I'm so glad you memorize commercials. This will really expand your mind!

MICHAEL. You wanna play or you wanna talk?

GABE. *(moves)* Watch your Quee-een.

MICHAEL. Ow! *(stumped)*

GABE. Great move, eh? A Boris Karpov move! Not an Eddie Fisher move!

MICHAEL. Bobby Fisher!

GABE. What's the difference?! *(moves)* Knight takes pawn. *(draws out the comment)* The tailor- goes after- the Kii-ing...but fii-irrst, he must get rid of the tzatzke yenta Queenele.

MICHAEL. Shh!

GABE. *(humming loud)* Ya-ba-ba-ba-ba-ba-ba-yay-ba-by-by-

MICHAEL. Do you mind!

GABE. I'm sorry. *(beat)* Ya-ba-ba-ba-ba-

MICHAEL. Ya-ba-da-ba-do Fred Flintstone! Do you have a tick, Zaydee?

GABE. A Hassidik tick, ya-ba-ba-ba-ba-ba-ba-ba-

MICHAEL. So annoying…

GABE. Shh, I'm memorizing the lyrics, ya-ba-ba-ba-ba

MICHAEL. Zaydee, I'm trying to think!

GABE. So think! I'm not stopping you from thinking. *(beat)* So,…how was school today?

MICHAEL. Go-ood.

GABE. What did you learn?

MICHAEL. No-thiiing.

GABE. You spend a whole day in school and learn no-thiiing?

MICHAEL. Zaydee, you're driving me nuts!

GABE. Okay, okay, okay, no more talking. *(beat)* You nervous about your Bar Mitzvah?… You should be nervous… not a lot…just a little…it's natural to be nervous…not a lot, but a-

MICHAEL. *(strong move)* There! Take that!

GABE. Oooh, very good, a baytzim attack! Never be afraid to lead with your baytzim! Balls and brains, that's what a man needs to survive in this world. A big heart, a big brain, and biiiig—

MICHAEL. Shhh!

GABE. That's how the Jew survived, a big heart, a big brain, and biiig –

MICHAEL. *(leaps out of chair)* THAT'S IT YENTA! I QUIT! *(Door buzzer sounds.)*

GABE. Sit down and lose like a man!

MICHAEL. Then button up!

GABE. I can't talk? I talk to Ali, he don't complain!

MICHAEL. I know what you're doing, Zaydee,

GABE. What am I doing?

MICHAEL. You're trying to break my concentration!

GABE. Just the opposite! I'm building up your concentration!

MICHAEL. How?

GABE. By being difficult! You learn the most from difficult people.

MICHAEL. Then, I'm learning a lot!

GABE. Sit down and finish the game!

MICHAEL. No!

GABE. I said, sit down!

MICHAEL. Will you be quiet?

GABE. I am quiet!

DIANE. *(walks in carrying a shopping bag)* Hey, hey, what's all the noise?

MICHAEL. Zaydee's doing his shtick!

GABE. He's losing, so he quits.

MICHAEL. I'm losing? You're the one losing!

DIANE. My, what a friendly game.

GABE. It's not a game, it's war!

DIANE. *(looking at the board)* Who's winning?

MICHAEL/GABE. I AM!!

MICHAEL. Check! *(slams his move)*

GABE. Oy! I got tzures! I'm in trouble!

DIANE. Gabe, why is it so important for an old man to beat a young kid?

GABE. You wouldn't understand. You're a woman, *(back to game)* Ay, yay, yaaay, this is not good, not good,

MICHAEL. You are in deep doo doo, Zaydee!

GABE. Tell your son to be quiet.

DIANE. Why don't you play checkers?

GABE. Checkers is for dummies! Chess is a game for the mind! *(suddenly gets up and walks away)* You're right Mamele, a game shouldn't be so important.

MICHAEL. Mom!

DIANE. Go back and finish the game!

GABE. I don't feel so good.

DIANE. What's wrong?

GABE. Alll of a sudden everything hurts me.

DIANE. All of a sudden?

GABE. My bones, my playtza, my back, my kop, something in my system, something in the air, something in something…

MICHAEL. Mom, look what he's doing!

DIANE. Finish the game!

GABE. *(whispers)* I can't let him beat me before his Bar Mitzvah! This was gonna be my Bar Mitzvah present to him! *(MICHAEL goes back to concentrating on the game.)* So, how was your day, Mamele?

DIANE. Great! I got some terrific news!

GABE. You're pregnant!?

DIANE. No, I'm not pregnant! I was accepted into the doctoral program at the Psychoanalytic Institute!

MICHAEL. *(jumps up, hugging her)* Wow! Congratulations, Mom!

DIANE. Thank you.

GABE. I'd be much happier if you were pregnant.

DIANE. I'm sure you would, Gabe.

GABE. You're still a young woman.

DIANE. Thank you for your vote of confidence.

GABE. I'll give you more than a vote. You have a baby, I give you two thousand dollars. I write you a check right now!

MICHAEL. Take it Mom! Take it!

DIANE. Two thousand dollars? That's it?

GABE. All right, make it three.

DIANE. Last week it was four.

GABE. Next week it'll be two, take the three!

MICHAEL. Take it, Mom! Take it!

GABE. Take it.

DIANE. Gabe, we have a nice family, why push it?

GABE. One child is not a family.

DIANE. It's not?

GABE. No. One child is a triangle. Two's a family. Four! Four thousand! My final offer!

DIANE. Gabe, you can't bribe someone to have a baby. You have to want it.

GABE. I do. Mamele, we lost over two million children.

DIANE. I know Gabe, but I'm only one woman. Come Michael, we have to go home to prepare for Shabbes!

MICHAEL. I can't leave now! I got 'em by the baytzim!

DIANE. MICHAEL! Where did you learn that?!

GABE. *(cuts in)* Listen to your mother! Go home, before I kill you!

MICHAEL. *(gets up)* Are we stopping off at Moishe's take-out?

DIANE. No. Tonight's a surprise.

MICHAEL. What Mom?

DIANE. It's a surprise.

MICHAEL. Come on, tell us!

DIANE. Okay. In celebration of your upcoming Bar Mitzvah and Dad coming home for the week-end, I cooked an old-fashioned Shabbes meal, not recommended by the American Heart Association. Challah, salad, chopped liver, chicken soup with noodles and kreplach, stuffed veal, brisket, Belgium carrots, and ruggelach for dessert!

GABE. Now that's what I call a Shabbes meal! I'm getting a heartburn just thinking about it!

DIANE. Not bad for a shikse, eh Gabe?

GABE. Boytschick, if it wasn't for your shikse mother, your father wouldn't know he's a Jew! I remember the first time your Poppa brought Momme home,

MICHAEL. Did you like her?

GABE. I loved her!

DIANE. Yeah! Zaydee, took one look at me n' almost put the chisel through his hand.

GABE. I wasn't expecting a beautiful looking blonde. I was hoping for a Gentile, that looked like a Jew, but you did a very nice thing for us that night.

DIANE. I did?

GABE. Yes, you brought us a raisin challah.

DIANE. It was Shabbes Gabe. What's Shabbes without a good challah.

GABE. Your mamma, she's an E-m'se Ay-shis Cha-yil!

MICHAEL. What's that?

GABE. A Woman of Valor. *(kisses her hand)*

DIANE. Oh that's so sweet Gabe. I waited fifteen years for this. But better late than never, right Michael?

MICHAEL. *(studying the chessboard)* Yeah, Zaydee's slow.

GABE. I'll give you slow! *(takes off after* **MICHAEL***)* You little Kaker!

MICHAEL. *(running away)* Mom, Zaydee made chicken soup!

DIANE. You did? Let me see!

GABE. *(chasing* **MICHAEL***)* Go home troublemaker!

DIANE. See you at seven.

MICHAEL. *(As they leave,* **MICHAEL** *makes one last move.)* Checkmate!

GABE. OY!!

MICHAEL. YES! *(fist in the air)*

(blackout)

Scene Two

(Shabbat dinner table is set in **STUART** *and* **DIANE**'s *dining room.* **DIANE** *brings in wine glasses, followed by* **GABE** *and* **MICHAEL**, *bringing in other items.)*

DIANE. It's after eight already.

GABE. Don't worry Mamele, I'm sure as soon as we start to eat, Stuart will come. It's like waiting for a bus. You wait, you wait, you get disgusted, you start to walk, it comes! Let's begin. *(***GABE*** and* **MICHAEL** *sit.)*

DIANE. *(places the kerchief on her head, lights the Sabbath candles)* Baruch Ata Adonai, Elohaynu Melech Ha-olam, Asher Kid'shanu B'mitzvotav V'tzeevanu L'hadlik Ner Shel Shabbes.

GABE AND MICHAEL. Amen.

GABE. *(stands, lifts the silver Kiddush cup and recites blessing over the wine)* Baruch Ata Adonai, Elohaynu Melech Ha-olam, Boray P'ree Ha-gafen!

GABE/DIANE/MICHAEL. Amen.

(Door slams. **STUART** *rushes in carrying his briefcase and a wrapped gift.)*

GABE. You see! I told you! Pappa's home!

STUART. I'm very sorry everyone.

MICHAEL. Hi Dad!

DIANE. Hi Honey.

STUART. Hi everyone! The meeting ran over, I just missed the shuttle flight, traffic was a mess, I am so sorry.

GABE. President Reagan's new speechwriter doesn't owe any apologies, unless you wrote a lousy speech.

STUART. That's not funny, Pop. One lousy speech, and I'm out.

DIANE. Is everything all right?

STUART. I got called into Executive Session.

GABE. Executive session, Poo, Poo!

DIANE. We're up to the Motzi.

STUART. *(puts on his Yarmulke, breaks off a piece of challah)* Blessed art thou o' Lord our God, King of the universe, who bringest forth bread –

GABE. *(cuts him off)* Wa, wa, wait a second! One month in Washington and you forgot the Hebrew Motzi? If I want the English Motzi, I'll call in Billy Graham.

STUART. Baruch Ata Adonai, Elohaynu Melech Ha-olam, Ha-motzi Lechem Min Ha-aretz.

ALL. Amen. *(**STUART** cuts the challah and passes it around.)*

GABE. Now that's a blessing! The schnapps, Boytschick. *(rises)* Attention! Attention! Ladies and Gentlemen! I want to make a toast! *(**MICHAEL** pours **ZAYDEE** a shot of scotch. **GABE** motions to add more.)* First of all, I want to toast myself, for having such successful children. To you, Stuart, my son the big shot, on your appointment to the White House. I wish you continued success!

STUART. Thank you.

GABE. To Mamele, good luck on being accepted for your Ph.D.!

STUART. You made it?! *(jumps out of the chair to kiss her)*

DIANE. I made it!

GABE. She made it! She made it! You're not the only smart one in the family!

STUART. That's terrific! I'm so happy for you!

GABE. *(to **MICHAEL**)* Your mother's going to be a doctor! Not an R.D., not a real doctor but a doctor nevertheless!

STUART. I am so proud of you, *(lovey dovey)*

DIANE. Thank you.

STUART. I know how hard you've worked for this,

DIANE. It really feels great,

STUART. And I'm sorry I was late, I know how important, Sabbath is for you –

DIANE. It's okay, honey,

STUART. I love you, so much.

DIANE. Love you too. *(They kiss.)*

GABE. Enough with the loving! You're married!! *(continuing the toast)* And finally to my pride and joy, my Boytschick, on your upcoming Bar Mitzvah!

MICHAEL. *(quickly)* And to Zaydee's Muhammad Ali! May he breathe freedom… FOR ALL!

ALL. Hear! Hear!

GABE. Children, we have a lot to look forward to and a lot to be thankful for. Mazel Tov to all, and I know Bubbee's watching with a smile from above. L'chayim!

ALL. L'chayim! *(They clink and drink.)*

DIANE. Chopped liver anyone? *(passing it around)*

MICHAEL. Uch!

GABE. This will really plug me up. Jewish cement!

DIANE. Try some Michael.

MICHAEL. It's gross!

DIANE. *(puts some on his plate)* Honey, it's delicious.

MICHAEL. It looks like poo!

DIANE. Michael!!

STUART. Guess what I have for Michael?

MICHAEL. What Dad?

STUART. Call it an early Bar Mitzvah present from Mom n' I! *(surprises MICHAEL with gift box)*

DIANE. Congratulations Michael.

MICHAEL. Wow! *(rnthusiastically tearing the wrapping)* Thanks, Dad, thanks, Mom. OH WOW! A NINTENDO! A NINTENDO! *(hugging STUART and DIANE)* A NINTENDO, ZAYDEE! A NINTENDO!! THEY GOT ME A NINTENDO!

GABE. Nintendo! Nintendo! Noch a TSCHATSCH-KI-YENDO! Let's eat! *(They settle in. STUART's fatigued.)* You tired, eh Stuart? *(STUART shrugs.)* You got a lot on your head. It's hard to work with your head, easier with the hands. That's why I sculpt, no headaches.

STUART. Yeah…

GABE. *(to* MICHAEL*)* That's what Commandant Mueller used to say in the concentration camp, he said, "I sculpt to take my mind off the...other things."

MICHAEL. Zaydee, tell the Mueller story!

STUART. Not again!

GABE. A true German artist! He murdered by day and sculpted by night.

STUART. Can we change the subject?

GABE. *(to* MICHAEL*)* Mueller taught me how to sculpt.

STUART. We know the story, Pop.

GABE. *(to* MICHAEL*)* Mueller saw I was young and strong and picked me out of a death march to shlep limestones from the quarry to his studio.

MICHAEL. What about the time he turned his back on you?

STUART. Hey, hey,

GABE. Oh yes! He turned his back! *(picks up the challah knife)* Then, I picked up a chisel –

MICHAEL. *(picks up the Challah knife!)* YEAAAH!

GABE. An inch from his neck,

STUART. Come on guys!

MICHAEL. His thick hairy neck,

GABE. His fat neck!

STUART. Hey! I'm trying to have some dinner here.

GABE. I'm telling a good story.

STUART. Well, could you tell another one without Nazis in it, please!

DIANE. Stuart, don't be disrespectful.

GABE. It's all right, I'm used to it.

STUART. I'm home five minutes and he's bringing up Nazis! Let him watch Hogan's Hero's!

GABE. I do! But what did I do, so terrible, I'm talking to Boytschick.

DIANE. Gabe, Stuart just got home, he's trying to unwind, give him a few minutes.

GABE. You're right. I'm sorry Stuart, I'm just happy to see you.

STUART. Well, try to contain your enthusiasm.

GABE. I'm just very excited to hear about your new job! (**STUART** *is eating.*) How is it going?… You got some job there eh, Stuart?

STUART. Yeah.

GABE. Can't be easy.

STUART. It's not.

GABE. Beginnings are always difficult.

STUART. And the middle, and the end.

GABE. It will get better with time.

STUART. Yeah…

GABE. So, listen, Boytschick wants you to speak in his school.

STUART. Pop, don't bug me!

GABE. I'm not bugging, but if your son –

STUART. Pop.

GABE. Asks you for a small favor, then –

STUART. POP! Can you not –

MICHAEL. *(cuts in to break the tension)* Eh, Dad, I got an A in Computer Science today. Only one in the class.

STUART. That's good, Michael, keep it up.

MICHAEL. Wanna see my paper?

STUART. Later. So what's with the Bar Mitzvah, are you ready?

MICHAEL. I'm ready, Dad.

STUART. Is he ready, Pop?

GABE. He's ready, Captain!

STUART. Did you two study Haftarah, or did you play chess?

MICHAEL. We –

GABE. Did both.

STUART. Both?

GABE. All right. We only did Haftarah. *(All laugh, except* STUART.*)*

STUART. You better know your Haftarah, Son.

GABE. He knows it. He knows it. Show 'em, Boytschick, show your Poppa.

STUART. It's okay, he doesn't have to show me.

GABE. Show 'em, show 'em-

STUART. It's all right.

GABE. Listen to this, Stuart. C'mon!

STUART. I said –

GABE. Go ahead, Boytschick.

MICHAEL. *(begins chant) (overlapping dialogue)* Baruch Ata Adonai…

STUART. I… I… look…

GABE. Terrific, terrific,

MICHAEL. Elohaynu Me-lech Ha-olam,

GABE. Wonderful,

STUART. I said I-

GABE. Ah, what a sweet voice,

MICHAEL. Asher Ba-char B'ni Vim Tovim,

STUART. STOP! I BELIEVE YOU!!

DIANE. Calm down, Stuart.

STUART. *(beat)* Is everything else set? *(takes out a check list)*

DIANE. All set. *(fields* STUART*'s question lightheartedly as she's tossing salad)*

STUART. The band?

DIANE. Set.

STUART. D.J.?

DIANE. Set.

STUART. Florist?

DIANE. Set.

STUART. Photographer's?

DIANE. Set.

STUART. Video?

DIANE. Set.

STUART. Caterer?

DIANE. Set.

STUART. Three entree's, prime, salmon, chicken,

DIANE. Stuart,

STUART. French service, international coffee bar, vodka bar,

DIANE. Stuart,

STUART. Viennese table,

DIANE. Stop it.

STUART. Theme?

DIANE. Theme?

STUART. Yes! What's the theme? Michael's Bar Mitzvah theme?

DIANE. The theme is Michael's Bar Mitzvah! Salad anyone?
   MICHAEL? *(tossing and serving salad)*

STUART. How about the seating?

DIANE. Stuart, it's Shabbes. Can we enjoy each other's company, please.

STUART. I just don't want you to forget anything.

DIANE. Stop worrying, it's all taken care of.

STUART. *(beat)* What about the seating?

DIANE. Can you believe how obsessed he is?

STUART. How did you arrange the seating?

DIANE. I put all your relatives who don't talk to each other at the same table!

   (All laugh, except **STUART.** *)*

STUART. I mean, the Washington table. Where did you put the Washington table? Next to us, I hope!

DIANE. I put Washington's finest next to the band and sat your Aunt Nora and Uncle Shmucky at their table!
   (laughing continues)

MICHAEL. Who's Uncle Shmucky?

DIANE. A distant cousin. Zaydee's called him Uncle Shmucky for so many years, we forgot his real name!

MICHAEL. Be careful you don't write "Uncle Shmucky" on the seat card!

DIANE. Can you imagine if I did?

MICHAEL. Who would pick up a card that says Uncle Shmucky?

GABE. Who else?

GABE/DIANE/MICHAEL. *(beat)* UNCLE SHMUCKY!!

GABE. Yeah Boytschick, every family has their own Uncle Shmucky. They go by different names, but we know who they are! *(more laughing)*

STUART. I'm so glad everyone's having a good time while I'm trying to have a serious conversation.

DIANE. Why? Is this a serious occasion?

STUART. I just want the function to be perfect, that's all.

DIANE. It'll be very nice, Stuart.

STUART. But, will it be perfect?

DIANE. It's a Bar Mitzvah, Stuart, not an Olympic event. Salad, Gabe?

GABE. Not for me.

DIANE. It's fresh.

GABE. It could be fresh. I don't like salad.

DIANE. I can take the mushrooms out.

GABE. It's not the mushrooms. It's the lettuce that bothers me. It has no taste.

DIANE. Lettuce isn't supposed to have taste. That's why you add dressing.

GABE. So, why not just eat the dressing?

DIANE. Then you don't get the greens.

GABE. Greens are for behaymus.

MICHAEL. What's behaymus?

GABE. Cattle.

DIANE. Another progressive man of his day!

GABE. Let me ask you something, Mamele. How long do cows live? Ten, twenty years? I lived a whole life, I never touched a piece of lettuce. Maybe if the behaymus stopped eating lettuce, they'd live to be my age!

(**GABE**, **DIANE**, *and* **MICHAEL** *laugh*.)

STUART. What about the Maitre d' and valet parking?

DIANE. Would you look how he can't stop!

STUART. The Maitre d', valet parking?

DIANE. Done.

STUART. Candle lighting?

DIANE. Stuart!

STUART. Who's doing the candles?

MICHAEL. Oh, Dad, it's so dumb and boring and no one pays any attention!

STUART. Who's lighting the first three candles?

MICHAEL. Dad, why don't you just welcome everyone. Light a candle for those who are alive. Another candle for those who are dead. Zaydee makes the Motzi, you make the toast, band plays "Hava Nagillah," DJ plays "Celebration", and HOP, PLOP, we're outta there!

(*momentary beat of silence as* **MICHAEL**'*s suggestion is considered*)

GABE. Sounds good to me!

STUART. Absolutely not!

MICHAEL. Why not, Dad?

STUART. Because that's not how it's done, Michael!

MICHAEL. But, Dad, it's my Bar Mitzvah.

STUART. It's not your Bar Mitzvah!

GABE/DIANE/MICHAEL. IT'S NOT?!

STUART. What I mean is… Michael plays an important part…

DIANE. An important part?!

STUART. Honey, there are many people to consider, you don't want to offend or overlook anyone, this occasion is…a…a,

GABE. A typical Bar Mitzvah. Another American-Jewish tragedy!

DIANE/STUART. Gabe!

GABE. I'm sorry, I'm sorry, pass the lettuce.

STUART. All I know is, the closer we get to the Bar Mitzvah,

GABE. The more nervayish you become.

STUART. I am not nervous, Pop! I'm excited!

GABE. You look nervayish to me.

STUART. *(pointing to* **MICHAEL***)* He's the one that should be nervous.

MICHAEL. That's what Zaydee said, not a lot, just a little.

GABE. I only said that to improve your performance.

STUART. It better be a good one, Son. I don't want to be embarrassed. I have many important people coming.

MICHAEL. Yes, Dad.

DIANE. *(beat)* Was that really necessary?

STUART. What?

DIANE. "Don't embarrass me, Son. I have many important people coming?!"

STUART. I do.

DIANE. So what?!

GABE. Children,

STUART. I can't have expectations of my own son?

DIANE. Not if it's to make you look good!

GABE. Children, don't argue.

STUART. It's to make all of us look good!

DIANE. It's not about looking good!

GABE. No fighting children.

STUART. What's wrong in looking good? What's wrong in showing off your best?

DIANE. The showing off part!

GABE. Children,

STUART. I can't be proud of what I achieved? We started with nothing, Diane!

DIANE. Who cares? That's for us to know. You don't impress anyone with a Bar Mitzvah, Stuart. People go to dozens of Bar Mitzvahs. One ice sculpture's like the next.

MICHAEL. No swans, Mom, please, no swans!

DIANE. No swans, Michael.

STUART. *(beat)* What's wrong with swans?

DIANE. Oh, Stuart,

GABE. Stuart,

MICHAEL. Dad,

STUART. Mel Rosen had swans.

DIANE. Mel Rosen's a moron!

STUART. Do you know what those swans cost?!

DIANE. Stuart, swans belong in a pond, not on a buffet table!

STUART. I like swans.

DIANE. They're ostentatious.

STUART. I think they look elegant.

DIANE. What do you know from elegant, you're in politics!

STUART. *(beat)* I want swans, Diane.

DIANE. Stuart,

STUART. Call the decorater and tell him I want swans!

MICHAEL. Dad, they're so cheesy!

STUART. I want swans.

MICHAEL. They melt.

STUART. I want swans Michael!

MICHAEL. But, Dad –

STUART. I WANT SWANS! CAN'T I GET WHAT I WANT?!

GABE. *(beat)* I'll sculpt the farkakte schvans.

STUART. Don't sculpt anything!

GABE. Not even Muhammad Ali?

STUART. Sculpt nothing!

DIANE. Slow down, Stuart.

STUART. Don't tell me to slow down!

GABE. Children, children,

DIANE. Stuart, we eat together one night a week, don't ruin it.

STUART. I'm ruining it?

GABE. It's Shabbes, children, it's Shabbes!

STUART. I'm ruining it.

GABE. No fighting on Shabbes, save it for the rest of the week.

STUART. How am I ruining it?!

GABE. Look, it's the Bar Mitzvah, it destroys family's.

MICHAEL. Cancel it.

STUART. Be quiet, Michael!

DIANE. Just answer one question for me, Stuart. You are so concerned about all the things I shouldn't forget, do you plan on being late for your own son's Bar Mitzvah?

STUART. No, I don't plan on being late!! I don't understand you! I just landed the job of a lifetime. Any other wife would be beaming with pride!

DIANE. I am. I'm very proud of you honey. You've done very well in your career, but now you're home. We're all equals around here...come to think of it...I rule! So who wants chicken soup?

*(**MICHAEL** and **GABE** raise hands quickly. **STUART**'s hand goes up slowly. **DIANE** exits.)*

STUART. She makes me crazy!

GABE. Come on, Stuart, you're home. It's Shabbes. Think about the Bar Mitzvah! The chandeliers, the diamonds, the tuxedos, the face lifts, the tzitzke lifts, the toches lifts, the stomache lifts, the ski lifts, everything's a lift, a war against gravity! Ah nechtige tog!

MICHAEL. What's that mean Zaydee?!

GABE. Futile!

MICHAEL. I love Yiddish!

GABE. Think of the Jello mold of Jerusalem in a sea of red horseradish! Everything red, like the Red Sea, full of

Gefilte Fish! This will be some Bar Mitzvah! A Donald McDonald Trump Bar Mitzvah!

MICHAEL. I'd trade it in for a pizza party.

GABE. Bar Mitzvah's today, they're like weddings. Nothing like when I was a Bar Mitzvah.

MICHAEL. Tell me about your Bar Mitzvah, Zaydee.

STUART. Oh Michael, you've heard it a dozen times.

GABE. Boytschick wants to hear it.

DIANE. *(sticking her head in from kitchen)* Who wants kreplach? *(All raise hands quickly.)*

(to **GABE***)* Real kreplach, Gabe!

STUART. What is she talking about, "real" kreplach?

GABE. *(gives* **MICHAEL** *a look)* I have no idea. So! It was on a cold Shabbes morning in December, in a shtetle, far, far away in Galicia, when I first became a Bar Mitzvah!

STUART. Here we go again!

(this section with pace and **MICHAEL** *cutting* **GABE** *off)*

MICHAEL. And your Poppa woke you at five o'clock in the morning,

GABE. That's right, he put me in a hot tub,

MICHAEL. A Vanna!

GABE. Vanna, then –

MICHAEL. He soaped you up and scrubbed you down, head to toe, with a soft brush,

GABE. It wasn't so soft,

MICHAEL. You never felt so clean in your life!

GABE. *(beat)* Can I tell my own story?

MICHAEL. It was a m'chaya! A pleasure!

GABE. It was a taa-ke a m'chaya! Now, can I tell my story?

MICHAEL. Continue.

GABE. So- *(beat)* Thank you!

MICHAEL. You're welcome.

GABE. So, then, I –

MICHAEL. Put on a fresh clean shirt,

GABE. Washed and ironed,

MICHAEL. The night before,

GABE. By my mother,

MICHAEL. Shayndle.

GABE. Aleha Ha-Sholom,

MICHAEL. May she rest in peace.

GABE. Aleha Ha-Sholom,

MICHAEL. Aleha Ha-Sholom

GABE/MICHAEL. Amen!

GABE. Theee-eeen –

MICHAEL. You put on woolen coats, fur hats, leather shoes,

GABE. And –

MICHAEL. Off you marched to the Shtiebel Shul.

GABE. A –

MICHAEL. One-room synagogue in a basement.

GABE. When we got there-

MICHAEL. A minyan was waiting!

GABE. I –

MICHAEL. Led the entire service by heart,

GABE. For Kiddush –

MICHAEL. You ate herring, fresh rolls n' schnapps

GABE. Then,

MICHAEL. The Rabbi pinched your cheek, you went to Cheder, Poppa went to peddle shmattes and the Gantze Megillah cost two rubles!

GABE. *(beat)* That's exactly how I remember it! *(**DIANE** enters and serves the soup.)*

MICHAEL. I love that story! How was your Bar Mitzvah Dad?

GABE. *(cuts in)* Oh, his Bar Mitzvah was something special.

MICHAEL. Did Zaydee scrub you down?

STUART. No, I took a shower.

MICHAEL. Did you lead the whole service?

STUART. Yes.

MICHAEL. Wow! Was he good Zaydee?

GABE. Excellent.

MICHAEL. Did you teach him?

GABE. No, the Rabbi did.

MICHAEL. Why didn't you teach him Zaydee?

GABE. I was a Communist then.

MICHAEL. Was Dad a Communist?

STUART. Stop it.

GABE. No. He was a Republican. I was a Communist and I raised a Republican. You figure it out.

MICHAEL. What are you now Zaydee?

GABE. Confused!

MICHAEL. What's a Communist? What do Communists do?

GABE. They go to meetings and don't believe in God.

MICHAEL. But you're Jewish, how can you be a Communist?

GABE. I wasn't religious then. I was a cultural Jew.

MICHAEL. What's a cultural Jew?

STUART. He's in it for the food.

GABE. You should talk.

STUART. No, you should talk.

MICHAEL. How can you not believe in God, Zaydee?

GABE. I believe in him like he believes in me!

MICHAEL. But how can you not,

GABE. Please Boytschick, I'm eating my soup! Umm delicious Mamele!

DIANE. Thank you.

GABE. But, it needs more salt. Otherwise it tastes like pishach.

DIANE. Thanks for the recipe, Gabe. Next time I'll use pishach for my broth, and you can add the salt!

GABE. It's fine, just the way it is. *(slurping loud)*

MICHAEL. You're really loud, Zaydee.

GABE. This is how you eat when you enjoy! Like a chazer! Umm, just like Momme used to make, eh Stuart?

STUART. Mm.

GABE. So, what's going on in the White House, Suart? It's busy there, no? *(beat)* What's the matter Stuart, you forgot how to talk? *(beat)* So, what's doing? Iran-Contra, Central America, the Soviets, Germany? Tell me something, give me some inside news.

STUART. Reagan lost his hearing aid.

GABE. I'm afraid that wouldn't help his comprehension.

STUART. Only I make jokes about my new boss.

GABE. That wasn't a joke.

STUART. If you have such a low opinion of the man, how come you voted for him?

GABE. I like him. The shmuck tries to do the right thing. He just doesn't know what it is.

STUART. He's much sharper than you think.

GABE. Oh yeah? So tell me, tell me something!

STUART. Please, Pop, no shop talk.

GABE. Very nice, I got a big shot son in the White House, and I have to get my news from CNN.

STUART. That's where Reagan gets his.

GABE. He's supposed to make the news, not watch it.

STUART. Reagan doesn't move without the polls.

GABE. I thought the idea of a President is to lead, not follow.

STUART. The idea is to avoid controversy.

GABE. So what controversy were you avoiding today?

STUART. Pass the salt.

GABE. What contro –

STUART. No more.

GABE. What controversy?

STUART. ENOUGH!

MICHAEL. *(jumps in)* You see, that's how he gets you Dad. He tschepes the hell outta you! But I got 'em good today!

STUART. You beat Zaydee?! (**MICHAEL** *nods proudly.*) I thought you said you studied your Haftarah?

MICHAEL. Eh –

GABE. He knows it Stuart. He knows it. He's a smart boy.

MICHAEL. I'm not a boy!

GABE. But you know it.

MICHAEL. I know it. But, I don't know what I'm saying.

GABE. Don't worry, the Rabbi will tell you.

DIANE. The Rabbi shouldn't have to tell you anything Michael. You should know what you're saying for yourself.

GABE. He'll find out later, leave 'em alone.

DIANE. But he doesn't know what he's saying.

GABE. Who does?

DIANE. But, I thought you're teaching him Hebrew.

GABE. I don't know Hebrew! I know Yiddish.

DIANE. But, I thought you knew Hebrew.

GABE. Why, do the goyim know Latin?

STUART. I hate that word!

GABE. Latin?!

STUART. Goyim!

MICHAEL. Don't worry Mom. I'll be good! I'll do a good job on my Bar Mitzvah!

DIANE. I don't want you to be good Michael. I want you to know what you're saying! Otherwise it's meaningless. Your Bar Mitzvah isn't a performance, it's an opportunity to learn and grow. *(Phone starts ringing)* Don't cheapen it with a flawless recitation you don't understand. Treat it with respect and caring, even if others don't. *(answers phone)* Hello?

STUART. *(to GABE and MICHAEL)* Did you hear what I heard? *(Phone conversation overlaps with table talk.)*

DIANE. You heard right Stuart! Hello? Who is this? Hello?!

STUART. I heard right?

MICHAEL. Dad

STUART. I heard right?!

GABE. Don't get upset.

DIANE. *(into phone)* What? Who?

STUART. She said I don't care about my son's Bar Mitzvah!

MICHAEL. That's not what she said, Dad.

STUART. That's what I heard!

GABE. Oh Stuart, that's ridiculous.

DIANE. *(into phone)* I'm sorry, we have a bad connection!

STUART. So what is she saying?

GABE. Nothing! She didn't mean nothing!

DIANE. Who is this?

STUART. What is she saying? What is she,

DIANE. *(puts hand over the phone)* Would you be quiet please! *(back to the phone)* Pat?… Pat who?… *(hands* **STUART** *the phone)* Pat Buchannan.

*(***STUART***, just before taking the phone, as an afterthought, removes his yarmulke.)*

STUART. Shh!…

GABE. *(yells towards the phone)* ANTESAAMIT!

STUART. SHHH!… No, shh to you Sir. We, we're just eh… passing the anti pasta around. *(gives* **GABE** *a menacing look)* Yes Sir… Yes Sir…absolutely…I understand, Sir… no problem, Sir.… *(hangs up) (to* **GABE***)* That was my boss! How dare you embarrass me like that! I have a high-powered respectable position with respectable professionals who I'm proud to be associated with, and if you don't like it –

GABE. *(cuts in)* I'm sorry, I'm sorry, I shouldn't be so hard on Buchannan. I heard he had an uncle who died in the camps.

STUART. He did?

GABE. Fell off the tower. *(***STUART*** checks his briefcase.)* It's a joke, Stuart, relax!

DIANE. What's wrong Stuart?

STUART. Reagan's called another briefing.

GABE. Did the Russians attack?

STUART. No, the Russians didn't attack!

GABE. So sit down and eat!

STUART. I'm not hungry! *(puts on his jacket)*

MICHAEL. Dad, please don't go.

DIANE. You have to leave right now? This minute?

GABE. Your wife cooked you a delicious Shabbes meal. Eat! Es!! Your soup's getting cold. Washington can wait five minutes.

(**STUART** *sits down.*)

DIANE. What's going on?

STUART. I'm not free to discuss it.

GABE. You're not free to discuss it. You're not free to talk to us?

STUART. No.

GABE. What are we spies Stuart? We're your family! Now what's going on?

STUART. *(beat)* Reagan's decided to visit Bitburg.

GABE. Bitburg?

MICHAEL. What's Bitburg Dad?

GABE. The reports said Bonn.

STUART. I know what the reports said!

MICHAEL. What's Bitburg?

GABE. So…why…Bitburg? (**STUART** *hesitating*)

MICHAEL. What's Bitburg?

GABE. You can't be serious,

MICHAEL. Mom, what's Bitburg?

GABE. *(explodes pointing to his tattooed number)* THIS! THIS IS BITBURG!!

STUART. It's a cemetery for German soldiers.

GABE. A cemetery for NAZIS!!

MICHAEL/DIANE. Nazis?

STUART. No, not Nazis.

GABE. Yes Nazis! Hitler's Nazis are buried in Bitburg!

DIANE. Is that true Stuart?

STUART. Diane, there are 2,000 headstones of regular German Army who had nothing to do with the Nazis! Only a handful are S.S. and they're in a section we won't be anywhere near!

GABE. Did you hear Mamele? Only a handful are Nazis.

MICHAEL. You shouldn't go if Nazis are buried there Dad.

GABE. Your son has more sense in his pinky than you have in your kop!

DIANE. I'm sure it's not that simple, Gabe.

STUART. That's right, Pop, there are political realities.

GABE. What political realities?!

MICHAEL. What would happen if you didn't go, Dad?

STUART. It's out of the question!

GABE. Why is it out of the question?

STUART. Cause I'm not conducting my career around your politics.

GABE. This is not politics!

DIANE. Gabe, they'll be other issues you won't like.

GABE. This is not another issue.

MICHAEL. You shouldn't go Dad.

GABE. How can you do this? (**STUART**, *silently picking at his food*) Answer me!

DIANE. Could you let him eat in peace?

GABE. Why?! He ruined my appetite, why should he eat?!

MICHAEL. You could get another job, Dad.

STUART. I don't want another job! Get him out of here.

GABE. He don't bother me.

STUART. You bother me!

DIANE. You both bother me, stop!

GABE. I ask a simple question, why is your President going to Bitburg?

STUART. Reagan's paying off a political debt to Kohl. All right?!

GABE. What debt?

STUART. Our missiles are in his country facing Moscow!

GABE. So, he's protecting his toches with our missiles.

STUART. Our toches! There's growing opposition to keeping our missiles in West Germany! Kohl needs this visit! And we need Kohl. Case closed!

GABE. But why must it be Bitburg?

STUART. Because that's what Kohl wants!

GABE. Screw Kohl!

STUART. Screw Kohl? Do I have to remind you what a destabilized Germany means?

GABE. Do I have to remind you who you are?

STUART. I know who I am! Look Pop, the whole thing's gonna take a few minutes. A short speech, a wreath, a snapshot, and we're outta there.

GABE. Stuart, there's Jewish blood under those stones.

STUART. Pop, this is not a Jewish issue!

GABE. Stuart, you are the child of a survivor!

STUART. This is between the United States and Germany!

GABE. This is about respect for your father!

STUART. What about your respect for me?

GABE. You should be ashamed of yourself!

STUART. Why Pop? Cause I don't agree with you?

GABE. Beause you don't know where you stand!

STUART. Of course, I should stand with you! Because you're my father?

GABE. Because you're a Jew!

STUART. I'm also your son! The son you were so proud of, only a few minutes ago!

GABE. That was then. This is now!

STUART. Exactly!

GABE. Who are you? I don't know you!

STUART. I'm not that complex Pop. You hold on. I move on.

GABE. Is that the message of your graveyard speech, Dr. Stern, move on?

STUART. My message is peace.

GABE. Forgive and forget.

STUART. Move on.

GABE. I have a terrifying thought Stuart, that with statesmen like you, the Jews will forget the Holocaust long before the Germans do.

STUART. I would take that. But you wouldn't. You need to hold on to the past, keep track of wars, holidays, events, deaths, anniversaries, every single moment that's a reminder of some injustice inflicted on Jews... As if every event since the creation of time is judged by the universal standard, "Is it good, or not good for the Jews?" Well, has it ever occurred to you that what's good for the Jews might not be good for anyone else!

GABE. If it's good for the Jews, you can bet it's good for everyone else. But more important, you can be it's right.

STUART. That is the kind of pompous arrogance I hate!

GABE. You hate being a Jew!

DIANE. Don't say that!

GABE. She's more of a Jew than you are!

DIANE. Stop it!

STUART. I don't hate being a Jew! I'm proud to be a Jew! I just want to get away from the past. It has nothing to do with me!

GABE. A Jew without a past is not a Jew! And if you can't stand the truth and you can't take the pain, then don't call yourself a Jew!

STUART. I'll call myself anything I want!

DIANE. Would you two stop it?!

STUART. Stop it? He forgets the war ended forty years ago!

GABE. Nothing ended Stuart. This war has no end! Forty years is a day! A thousand years is a day!

STUART. Michael, get my coat.

GABE. I did not survive to forgive and forget!

STUART. We're not going there to forgive and forget. We're going to recognize what Germany's accomplished.

GABE. What has Germany accomplished Stuart? They made a Volkswagen? A Beetle? Design a cute car and the world will forgive you?!

STUART. Excuse me. I have a meeting to attend. *(checking the papers in his briefcase)*

GABE. Have they grieved? Have they torn themselves apart like the millions they tore apart?

STUART. Diane, I'm sorry about dinner, I have to go.

GABE. That's it? Nothing I said matters?

STUART. What do you want me to do?

GABE. Tell him!!

STUART. Tell who?

GABE. Your President!

STUART. Tell him What?!

GABE. Tell him butchers don't deserve burials! Tell him forgiveness comes from the victim! Tell him not to go!

STUART. You tell him!

GABE. Stuart, I'm begging you, please, don't let them do this. It's wrong. It's so wrong.

STUART. Listen to me Pop! I don't set policy. Not only don't I set policy, but I don't even open my mouth! I write! I write what they tell me to write!! That's my job!! I listen and I write!

GABE. You don't think?

STUART. I don't think Pop! I write what they think!

GABE. But what do you think when you don't write?!

DIANE. Leave him alone Gabe!

GABE. Leave him alone?? He sounds like a Nazi! He's just following orders!!

STUART. GET OUT OF MY HOUSE!!

DIANE. No Stuart no!

GABE. Listen to me Stuart and you better listen good. You tell your President, this, this…PUTZ, who served his country in Hollywood memorizing scripts in a soldier's uniform while American boys were dying! You tell this impostor, this, this…SHMUCK, that if he goes to Bitburg, he will have pissed on every Jew! Every Jew who ever lived or who ever died for being a Jew! And you Stuart, my son, may justify this in any way you wish, but THIS Jew, THIS time, will NOT stand for it!! NO! GOD HELP ME, THIS TIME, I WON'T! LOZ MIR AROYS! LOZ MIR AROYS!!

(Bolts out, slams door. **DIANE**, **STUART**, *and* **MICHAEL** *look at each other.)*

DIANE. Good Shabbes.

(DIANE *blows out the candles. Blackout.)*

End of Act One

ACT TWO

Scene One

(In pitch black darkness, phone rings.)

STUART. You have reached the home of Dr. Stuart and Diane Stern. Please leave a message and thank you for calling.

GABE. Hello, hello, pick up, pick up! Where are you? Why are you never home? Do you live there or do you just keep a machine! Talking to a machine! Machines talking to each other! A meshugene world with machines. Listen machine, tell your boss and the Misses I'm okay. Okay? I'm okay. Boytschick's okay. You're okay. We're all okay! Okay? Okay, be well. Good-bye. Wait! Don't hang up machine. *(beat)* Eh Stuart, this is your Poppa, and I... took Boytschick to Bitburg. Okay? Okay. Oh, and Stuart, I charged it on your American Express, okay?... Okay... Be well, regards to Mamele... Oh boy... *(hangs up)*

(Lights come up slowly on Bitburg cemetery on a cold, dreary, Saturday morning. EGON, a young German security guard is placing flowers on the graves, rows of white crosses. GABE and MICHAEL hide in the shadows, behind a tree, wearing their prayer shawls and holding prayer books. MICHAEL is kneeling, serving as the lookout.)

(jarring loudspeaker announcement)

ANNOUNCEMENT. (*voiceover*)

> FER-LASSEN-ZIE DIE-ZEN PLATZ ZO-FORT!!
> VIER VIEDER-HOLEN!
> ZIE MUSSEN DIE-ZEN PLATZ VER LASSEN!!

> LEAVE THIS AREA!!
> YOU MUST LEAVE THIS AREA!
> WE REPEAT, LEAVE THIS AREA!
> ZIE MUSSEN DIE-ZEN PLATZ VER-LASSEN!!

> (**EGON** *exits.* **MICHAEL** *and* **GABE** *come out of hiding.* **GABE** *is holding up a sign:* MISTER PRESIDENT YOUR PLACE IS WITH THE VICTIMS!*)*

GABE. So, Boytschick, when President Reagan and Chancellor Kohl march in with the big shots –

MICHAEL. We hold up the sign to Reagan and shout, "Mister President your place is with the victims"

GABE. You sound like a mouse! Can you sound like a lion?! Put some oomph into it!

MICHAEL. MISTER PRESIDENT! YOUR PLACE IS WITH THE VICTIMS!

GABE. AH! That's gut! His other eardrum should bust! Now finish up your Haftorah.

> (**MICHAEL** *stands up on the bench.*)

MICHAEL. Al-Ha-Kol Adonai

> Elo-haynu A-Nachnu Modim Lach
> Um'vorchim Otach Yit Barach…
> (*slows to a stop*) Simcha…B'fi…Kol-chai… Eh… Zaydee?

GABE. Yes?

MICHAEL. Who are we doing this for? There's no one here, no one's watching.

GABE. God is watching.

MICHAEL. You don't believe in God.

GABE. That doesn't mean he's not watching. Finish up!

MICHAEL. Al Hakol Adonai Eloheinu
 A Nachim Modim Lach
 Um'Vor'Chim Otach
 Yit Barach Shimch B'Fi Kawlchai
 Tamid L'olam Va-ed
 Baruch Ata Adonai
 M'Kadesh Ha-Shabbat!

GABE. Amen! Very nice! Very nice! I taught you good. How do you feel?

MICHAEL. Good Zaydee, I feel good.

GABE. Like an American Indian?

MICHAEL. Like a man! We made it Zaydee!

GABE. You made it Boytschick!

MICHAEL. Yes!

GABE. I'm so proud of you Boytschick! *(big hug)*

MICHAEL. Eh Zaydee,… now that I'm a man could you not call me Boytschick?

GABE. What should I call you Mantschick?

MICHAEL. Call me Michael.

GABE. Okay. No more Boytschick. From now on it's Michael.

MICHAEL. Thank you.

GABE. You're welcome. So, Boytschick, oops, Michael. Michael… So Michael, this is the part in Shul when the Rabbi speaks and everyone else falls asleep. Well, we're not exactly in Shul here, and I'm certainly not a Rabbi, but I'll do my best to say something, so you'll remember this occasion. Although, a protest Bar Mitzvah in Bitburg would be hard to forget… So, what should I tell you? I'll tell you exactly what my Poppa told me, *(beat)* Nothing!

MICHAEL. Nothing?

GABE. My Poppa didn't talk much. He was a tailor. If he opened his mouth, the pins would fall right into his stomach.

MICHAEL. Come on Zaydee, give me some words of wisdom.

GABE. Words of wisdom are drek! What you just did, is worth more than all the words! You performed a mitzvah! A good deed! A courageous act! You gave the martyrs dignity and you gave me hope!

MICHAEL. Okay, Okay, but do you have any advice for me?

GABE. What did I just do?

MICHAEL. That was a speech. The Rabbi always gives the Bar Mitzvah boy some advice.

GABE. You don't need advice from an old man.

MICHAEL. Yes I do, Zaydee. Make it my Bar Mitzvah present.

GABE. Well, in that case…what should I tell you Michael… you're a wonderful boy, a smart boy, clever, n' bright, n' brave, n' quick, n' handsome like a movie star! You remind me so much of…ME! Oy mein k'nd, you give me so much naches. You're a special child, a sweet child, blessed with a sweet soul, a gentle spirit, and a good heart, which will only grow as you grow…

MICHAEL. Is this what you told my dad?

GABE. Give me your keppy.

(**MICHAEL** *bows his head under* **GABE**'s *hands.*)

Yi-v're-ch'cha Adonai V'yis Ma-re-cha

Ya-er Adonai Pa-nav Ayle-cha V'Cho Necho Yiso Adonai Dan V'Alecho

V'ya-sem L'cha Shalom.

May God shine his light on you and grant you peace, Amen.

MICHAEL. Thank you Zaydee.

(**GABE** *kisses* **MICHAEL**'s *head. They sit down on the bench,* **GABE** *rubbing his feet.*)

GABE. Oy! My p'deshves are killing me. *(shudders from the cold)* A bissel chilly here, no?

MICHAEL. It's cold…

GABE. *(pulls out a flask from his jacket)* The same draft from my apartment follows me wherever I go. New York, Germany. I can never warm up. *(opens the flask)* I need a little fire for my pipik. L'Chaim!

MICHAEL. L'Chaim!

GABE. *(takes a swig)* Ah! That's good! But it went right down to my toes! One more! *(takes a second swig)*

MICHAEL. *(watching)* Oh, eh, Zaydee…how about a little schnapps for ol' Mantschick here?

GABE. Oh no, no, no, no,…

MICHAEL. I'm cold too, you know.

GABE. No, no, no!

MICHAEL. Fire for my pipick!

GABE. Your pipick's too young!

MICHAEL. You said I was a man!

GABE. Yes but,

MICHAEL. Men drink right?!

GABE. Yes, but,

MICHAEL. Am I a man or not?! Did I come here with you or not?!

GABE. *(pause)* If you tell your mother, I kill you!

MICHAEL. And my father?

GABE. Him, I'm not afraid of.

MICHAEL. *(whispers in his ear)* Zaydee, this is just between us, our little secret, stick with me and you don't have to worry.

GABE. *(beat)* For a young kid, you got some balls.*(pours* MICHAEL *a capful)* You can't say a word until you're married and out of the house. By then I should be dead! *(gives it to him)* Now drink it nice n' slow…

(**MICHAEL** *downs it quickly, seized by a coughing fit.*)

What are you m'shugeh?! It took me fifty years to drink like that!

MICHAEL. How do you drink this crap?!

GABE. It's Chivas Regal!

MICHAEL. Uch! It tastes horrible!

GABE. Who drinks for taste?! *(beat)* Not easy being a man, huh?

MICHAEL. *(while coughing)* Another shot.

GABE. What?

MICHAEL. I want another shot! Quick! Before I die!

GABE. Okay, we do it like this. I drink first, then leave you a drop, to smack your lips. *(He downs a shot.* MICHAEL *dips his finger in the cap, licks his finger and repeats.)*

MICHAEL. This is like doing the ten plagues at the Passover Seder. C'mon Zaydee don't baby me.

(GABE *pours a slight amount,* MICHAEL *sips it, makes a face.)*

GABE. You want some herring and Challah, to soak up the shnapps!

MICHAEL. No thank you, I'll pass. See Zaydee, I can drink. It's no big deal drinking shnapps, you just gotta get used to it.

GABE. Yes, for us Alte Kahkers it's a required taste *(takes another swig) (silence as they scan the cemetery)* Look at this place…

MICHAEL. It's creepy…

GABE. *(stands up)* The scum of the earth lie here…even the fresh air stinks.

MICHAEL. You scared Zaydee?

GABE. Nah…you?

MICHAEL. No way… well… maybe a little…

GABE. Don't worry, mein kind, nothing will happen to you. As long as I'm here, nothing will happen to you…

MICHAEL. *(pause)* How long do we have to wait?

GABE. *(suddenly)* Shh!

MICHAEL. What?…

GABE. Shh,… listen…

MICHAEL. I don't hear anything.

GABE. Listen…

MICHAEL. It's the wind.

GABE. No… they're here,

MICHAEL. Who?

GABE. The Devils…

MICHAEL. What Devils?

GABE. The Devils! The Devils! *(reading the gravestone names)* Guttenberg!… Freuhoffer!… Becker!… Mueller, where's Meuller? Where's Mueller?

MICHAEL. Mueller?

GABE. *(goes into a frenzy)* MUELLER! THE MURDERER! MUELLER!

MICHAEL. There's no Mueller here…

GABE. STEP ON THEM! STEP ON THEM! STEP ON THEIR GRAVES! *(grabs **MICHAEL***'s hands*)* WE WON BOYTSCHICK! WE WON! LOOK MOMME, ROCHEL, WE WON! WE DANCE ON THEIR GRAVES! COME MICHAEL, WE DANCE FOR MOMME, ROCHEL! *(spins **MICHAEL** around)* SIM N'TOV N' MAZEL TOV N' MAZEL TOV N' SIM N'

MICHAEL. *(getting freaked out)* Zaydee, stop, please, stop, stop,

GABE. SIM N' TOV N' MAZEL TOV N' MAZEL TOV N' SIM N' TOV, SIM N' TOV N' MAZL TOV N' MAZEL TOV N' SIM N' TOV SIM N' TOV N'

*(**MICHAEL** breaks free, clearly shaken, slumps down)*

Oy, what did I do? I pull a young child into my tzures.

*(sits down next to **MICHAEL**, puts his arm around him)*

I called your Momme n' Poppa last night.

MICHAEL. You did?

GABE. Yes.

MICHAEL. Were they angry?

GABE. No, how could they be angry with you?

MICHAEL. What did they say?

GABE. They weren't home, I left a message.

MICHAEL. You told them we were here?

GABE. Yes.

MICHAEL. Don't worry Zaydee I'll tell 'em it was all my fault.

GABE. You love your Zaydee?

MICHAEL. Do I have a choice?

GABE. Give me a squeeze. (MICHAEL *hugs* GABE.) Oy, not so hard, I don't feel so good. *(clutches his chest)* Oh! Oh!

MICHAEL. Oh my God! Zaydee are you having a heart attack?!

GABE. No, I only give heart attacks, but now, I got such a heart burn and headache!

MICHAEL. You drank too much!

GABE. Shah! Be quiet, I have to give a greps! *(Belches)*

MICHAEL. Feel better?

GABE. I'm nausening!

MICHAEL. You want some Alka Seltzer?

GABE. You brought Alka Seltzer?

MICHAEL. *(gets Alka Seltzer out of his bag)* Sure. It's your favorite drink after schnapps!

GABE. My grandson's a doctor!

MICHAEL. It's called traveling with Zaydee!

GABE. Oooh, I could also use a good farts! Lufthansa's salty peanuts got me all farshtoppt! They give an old Jew with high blood pressure salty peanuts. Besterds are still trying to kill me. Oy, mine kop!

MICHAEL. I also brought Tylenol.

GABE. I take Excedrin.

MICHAEL. I don't have Excedrin!

GABE. I don't like Tylenol!

MICHAEL. Why?

GABE. The pills look too happy!

MICHAEL. You'll take what I got!

GABE. All right, all right, I'll take, I'll take.

*(**MICHAEL** gives **GABE** the Tylenol, as they both watch the Alka Seltzer fizz in water.)*

Now this is what I call a doctor with a prescription! Two Alka's and two Tylenol. A Jewish Boilermaker! L'Chayim!

MICHAEL. L'Chayim!

GABE. *(downs the Alka Seltzer and lets out a big belch)* Ahh! That was good!

MICHAEL. Don't fart Zaydee!

GABE. You afraid I'll wake up the dead?

MICHAEL. I'm afraid you'll kill me! *(beat)* Zaydee when we get home, do you think I'll be grounded?

GABE. What are you an airplane?!

MICHAEL. I'm serious!

GABE. Boytschick, if they ground you, they have to ground me! *(beat)* Believe me Michael, I wouldn't hurt your parents for anything in the world, but I couldn't just do nothing.

MICHAEL. No, you had to do something.

GABE. Otherwise the martyrs die for nothing…then what are we?

MICHAEL. Right.

GABE. It's up to us who remain, to live for them, fight for them, you understand?

MICHAEL. Yes.

GABE. So it can, never, happen again!

MICHAEL. Never!

GABE. You must never forget!

MICHAEL. I won't.

GABE. Never forget you're a Jew. A Jew first. Then you can be whatever the hell you want to be! American, French, but a Jew first!

MICHAEL. Yes Sir!

GABE. And Jews take no crap!

MICHAEL. No sir!

GABE. We took enough!

MICHAEL. How much can you take?!

GABE. Let someone else take it!

MICHAEL. Let someone else take it!

GABE. That's my lesson for today!

MICHAEL. Good!

GABE. Kaddish!

MICHAEL. Kaddish!

GABE. For the millions and millions of innocents, we pray…

(GABE *and* MICHAEL *pray with fervor.*)

GABE/MICHAEL. Yis-ga-dal v'yis kadash she'me raba. B'alma dee'vra k'roo-tay. Va-yimlach malchoo-tay b'ha-ye-hon uv'yaw-mey-hon,

EGON. (*re-enters, startling* GABE *and* MICHAEL) Sir!! The announcement stated this area is strictly off limits.

GABE. (*resolute*) Yis-ga-dal v'yis kdash she'me raba. B'alma dee'vra k'roo-tay.

EGON. Please gather your belongings and leave!

GABE/MICHAEL. Va-yimlach malchoo-tay b'ha-ye-how ovlyaw-mey-chon.

EGON. Did you hear the announcement?

GABE/MICHAEL. Uv'cha-yeh d'chol be yisrael.

EGON. Antschuldig zie bitte!

GABE/MICHAEL. Ba-ga-lah uv'zman koreev v'imroo A-men!

EGON. Verlassen Sie Diezen Platz! Leave!

GABE. (*to* EGON) Say Amen!

EGON. Eh…Amen.

GABE/MICHAEL. Y'hay-shme raba m'vor-ach l'olam ul'ol-may, all-my-ya!

EGON. Sir, stop it!

GABE/MICHAEL. Yit-ba-rach, v'yit-ta bach, v'yit pa-ar, v'yit ro-mam, v'yit-na-sey.

EGON. (*reaches out and touches* GABE*'s prayer shawl*) Please respect our grounds!

GABE. Take your filthy hands off my Talis!

EGON. Then please leave!

GABE. Are you crazy? Do you know what I had to go through to get here? I had to fly Lufthansa!

EGON. Sir,

GABE. *(cuts off* **EGON***)* Seven hours of Germans speaking German –

EGON. Sir I –

GABE. Seven hours of *(mocking sound sucking up phlegm)*

EGON. Sir, I must ask –

GABE. And do you know what else dem Lufthansa besterds did?

EGON. Please, sir –

GABE. They charged me full price for a child!

MICHAEL. I'm not a child!

GABE. For discounts you are!

EGON. Sir,

GABE. At least with El-Al you can bargain.

EGON. Sir, please take the boy –

MICHAEL. I'm not a boy!

EGON. Take the boy and leave!

GABE. We're not finished!

EGON. We'll see. *(takes out his Walkie Talkie)*

MICHAEL. Hey, Officer, what's the problem? We're not bothering anyone. We're protesting our President.

EGON. Then do it on your soil young man. Don't do it here.

MICHAEL. No Sir! W're doing it here! *(gives* **GABE** *a high five)* I told him!

*(***EGON*** turns his back, talking on his Walkie Talkie.)*

GABE. Go on arrest us Mr. Gestapo!

MICHAEL. Yeah! Arrest us!

GABE. Look at this Michael, a Jew can't get arrested in Germany! Forty years ago I wouldn't even have to ask.

EGON. If you don't leave, you will be arrested.

GABE. Good! That's just what we want! *(to* **MICHAEL***)* He thinks this is 1941. *(to* **EGON***)* It's 1985 my friend and the world is watching. Oh, will this make a picture for CNN! An old Jew being dragged out of a Nazi cemetery! Ho! Ho! Larry King will have a ball with this!

*(***EGON*** is visibly perturbed.)*

MICHAEL. Don't rub it in Zaydee, we got 'em pissed off enough.

GABE. Why you think I'm afraid of him? *(to* **EGON***)* You think I'm afraid of you? What is your name Mister?

EGON. Egon Schmidt, Sir.

GABE. Ever seen a Jew before Schmidty?

EGON. Yes.

GABE. I mean a Jew who's not afraid?

EGON. Yes Sir.

GABE. THIS Jew is not afraid! *(pushes* **MICHAEL** *forward)* And THIS little Jew is not afraid!

MICHAEL. I'm not a little Jew!

GABE. We keep coming back Schmidty.

EGON. Sir-

MICHAEL. Yeah Schmidty, we keep coming back!

GABE. No matter what you do to us!

MICHAEL. We fight back!

GABE. The mouse that roared!

MICHAEL. The elephant!

GABE. Because now we have a state!

MICHAEL. A Jewish state!

GABE. Israel!

MICHAEL. A very Jewish State!

EGON. I know.

GABE. ISRAEL!

EGON. SIR!

GABE. You know Israel?

EGON. I know Israel!

GABE. How do you know Israel? You have relatives there?

EGON. Sir! President Reagan will be arriving shortly with Chancellor Kohl.

GABE. Good. Let them both drop dead! And I'll do the burial!

EGON. Sir, they must come through without interference.

GABE. Let them come, eh Boytschick?

MICHAEL. Let 'em come!

GABE. COME ON SHLEPPERS!!

MICHAEL. COME ON SHLEPPERS!!

GABE/MICHAEL. COME ON SHLEPPERS!!

EGON. *(picks up* **MICHAEL***'s backpack)* Please take your things and leave!

MICHAEL. Hey, that's my stuff! *(grabs hold of the bag and rips it free the moment* **STUART** *and* **DIANE** *enter)*

DIANE. Michael.

MICHAEL. Mom, dad!

GABE. Ah, the U.N. peace-keeping force just arrived!

DIANE. Michael, are you all right?

MICHAEL. I'm fine, Mom,

STUART. Are you hurt, son?

MICHAEL. No, I'm good, dad, really.

GABE. The Nazi was confiscating Boytschick's peckele!

EGON. Sir, it is my duty to clear the area.

STUART. I understand Officer. I'm Dr. Stern from the President's office.

EGON. Authorization papers.

*(***STUART*** gives ***EGON*** papers.)*

EGON. Danke.

GABE. *(to* **MICHAEL***)* We didn't need no stinkin' authorization papers.

*(***EGON*** is examining the papers.)*

STUART. *(takes* EGON *aside)* I need a few minutes with my father.

*(*EGON *returns the papers and exits.* GABE *waves protest sign towards* EGON.*)*

DIANE. You have some nerve Gabe!

GABE. Don't be upset Mamele.

DIANE. Don't Mamele me! Where do you come off kidnapping Michael?!

GABE. I didn't kidnap. I called you! Didn't you get the message?

DIANE. The message which said, "Don't worry I took Boytschick to Bitburg?!" Yes, we got that message!

MICHAEL. Mom, it's not Zaydee's fault! I asked to come. I wanted to do something important! Something I could tell my friends about!

DIANE. *(sniffing, cups* MICHAEL*'s face)* Michael, have you been drinking?

MICHAEL. Uhh…

DIANE. Is this what you want to tell your friends? How I learned to drink in Bitburg?!

GABE. I gave 'em a little schnapps.

DIANE. Stuart, he gave Michael whiskey! He's got him drinking in a cemetery!

MICHAEL. I was cold Mom.

DIANE. Then put on a sweater!

MICHAEL. I had one shot!

DIANE. Michael David Stern, don't give me any lip! I am not in the mood!

STUART. What are you doing here?

GABE. Saying Kaddish, his Haftorah.

STUART. *(picks up prayer book)* You did Michael's Bar Mitzvah here?! You use my son's Bar Mitzvah for your protest?

MICHAEL. It was practice, Dad, for next week.

GABE. Next week is a carnival. This is the real thing!

STUART. Good. So now that you both accomplished what you wanted, we can all go home. *(*MICHAEL *slowly gathers his things.* GABE *doesn't.)* Pop?… There are other protests, demonstrations in New York, Washington, Bergen Belsen, The President is going to Bergen Belsen. We can go there from here if you want.

GABE. So the putz is trading off graves. A death camp for a Nazi cemetery.

STUART. You don't want to go to Bergen Belsen?

GABE. Not especially.

STUART. Fine! Then there are two hundred and fifty thousand gathering at the U.N. Plaza tomorrow.

GABE. So go.

STUART. We can make it if you leave now.

GABE. I'm not going anywhere!

DIANE. Elie Wiesel is speaking.

GABE. He already spoke. Read the sign. He said, "Your place is with the victims!" Did your President listen? No! Nancy, the yenta, packs his underwear and they still come!

STUART. Last time, Pop. Are you leaving?

GABE. Not until I spit in your President's face.

MICHAEL. C'mon, Zaydee, you promised! You said we'd do the Bar Mitzvah, the Haftarah, and we leave.

GABE. But they're not here yet. The putz n' the Nazi, Frick n' Frack, they're not here yet!

STUART. And they won't be. Not until you're gone.

GABE. What?

STUART. Did you really think two governments would stand idly by and allow an old man with his grandson to sneak into a highly restricted security zone? You're being watched Pop, since you got here! Who do you think you're fooling? You call this a protest? It's a joke! If it weren't for me you would have been dragged out of here, already.

GABE. So all this is for nothing? You make me out to be a fool?

STUART. What do you think I look like?

GABE. That putz used me?

STUART. No one used you!

GABE. That putz Reagan used me for his political pawn! And you, you go behind my back?

STUART. I went behind your back?!

GABE. I will not have it!

STUART. Don't start!

GABE. I will not have it!!

DIANE. Gabe, calm down!

GABE. I WILL NOT HAVE IT!

DIANE. You'll get a stroke!

GABE. STROKE?! I'M GOING ON STRIKE!

(sings Yiddish resistance song, marching, overlapping dialogue)

GABE. Zog nisht kayn mol
　　　Az die gayst dem letztn vayg,

STUART. What are you doing?

GABE. Hotch him-len bly-ye-ne
　　　Farshtelin bloya-teg,

STUART. Stop it!

GABE. Ku-men Vet Noch
　　　Unzer Oys-g'benk-te shaw,

STUART. What are you accomplishing?!

GABE. S'vet A Poyk Ton
　　　Unzer Trot Mir
　　　Zeiven Daw!

STUART. Who are you defending?

GABE. Zog nisht kayn mol,
　　　Az die gayst dim letztn vayg

STUART. You're fighting for your dead. And they're fighting for their dead!

GABE. Hotch him-len bly-ye-ne farshtelin bloye teg…

STUART. But it's all about the dead!! Don't you see that?

GABE. *(stops)* And in your eyes, it's all equal!

STUART. No, it's not all equal. It can never be equal! Look Pop, Bitburg may have been a bad idea, but it's here, it's done, it's over. Can you let it go?

GABE. No! I can not let it go. I will not let it go!

STUART. Do you know what you've done to me? You cost me my job! They're just waiting for this to be over. I will have lasted five weeks in a job I worked my entire life for.

GABE. *(to DIANE)* He worries about a job.

DIANE. I think you should pack up and leave.

GABE. I think you should all drop dead! *(stunned silence)* What do you want from me! I'm a survivor. There's no way out!

STUART. *(pointing to the exit)* That's the way out Pop! You take yourself out! My God, when does it end? We're going on two generations! *(pointing to MICHAEL)* Three! You want me to feel the way you feel. I can't! You want me to be you. I'm not. YOU went through the Holocaust, I didn't! Give me a chance…Did you survive so you could pass on your bitterness?

GABE. I wasn't bothering no one Stuart. I was quiet. Momme died, I was quiet. Forty years I was quiet. I sat and chiseled my stone, didn't ask nothing from nobody. I took what little was left and tried to make a life, build a home, a family, do my work, my art… and then Bitburg! You give me Bitburg!

STUART. I didn't give you Bitburg!

GABE. Couldn't you stand with me? Show some courage!

STUART. *(silent)*

GABE. Aah, you're a disgrace to your own son!

MICHAEL. Don't say that Zaydee!

GABE. What does he teach you?

MICHAEL. Everything!

GABE. Nothing! He teaches you nothing!

MICHAEL. That's not true!

GABE. I teach you! I teach you History! I teach you Chess! Haftarah! Ali!

STUART. Who taught me Pop?

GABE. I teach you how to fight! How to stand up! How to be a man!

STUART. Who taught me?

GABE. That's why you're here with me!

STUART. Who taught me?

GABE. To prove you're a man, right?

MICHAEL. *(silent)*

GABE. RIGHT?!

MICHAEL. *(silent)*

GABE. Oh, go with your father!

MICHAEL. What did I do?

GABE. Leave me alone!

MICHAEL. Why are you mad at me?

GABE. Let him teach you!

MICHAEL. Can't you both teach me?

GABE. No!

MICHAEL. What are you doing Zaydee, it's like you're making me choose!

GABE. That's right! That's what a man does. He chooses. Right or wrong. Weak or strong!

STUART. Get your things Michael.

GABE. *(forces on MICHAEL a marker and paper)* Write, Michael! "All Germans Are Nazis."

EGON. *(enters)* Welcome to Bitburg Dr. Stern.

GABE. "All Germans Are Nazis."

EGON. The ceremony is delayed 30 minutes.

GABE. "All Germans are Nazis."

EGON. It can be less than 30 minutes.

GABE. Write, big letters! "All Germans Are Nazis"

EGON. That is uncalled for.

GABE. Why, do I offend you?

EGON. Very much, Sir.

GABE. I offend you? What do you call this?

EGON. Regular German Wehrmacht soldiers lie here, Sir.

GABE. Where are your S.S. buried?

EGON. Not here. *(tidying up the flowers)*

GABE. Do the S.S. get flowers too?

EGON. There were many divisions of S. S. Sir. Not all were murderers. But since you accuse us all, you should know your history better.

GABE. You see Michael, there are good Nazis and bad Nazis, and the good Nazis lie here and the bad Nazis-

EGON. There are distinctions, Sir!

GABE. I make no distinctions! Write Michael, "All Germans Are Nazis!"

STUART. Don't you dare!

GABE. Do it!

DIANE. Don't, Michael!

*(**GABE** shoves the marker into **MICHAEL**'s hand.)*

GABE. Write! "All Germans are Nazis!" Write, Michael, write, write, "All Germans-

STUART. *(grabs the sign and rips it)* Who are you to teach Michael anything!

GABE. Control yourself Mr. Diplomat.

STUART. Filling his head with poison!

GABE. Control.

STUART. He's not your son Pop! He's my son! You had your chance!

GABE. Oh, I wasn't a good father?

STUART. You were wonderful.

GABE. I didn't provide, I didn't protect?

STUART. "I will show you how to be a man"

GABE. You walked around naked, hungry?

STUART. Why don't you tell him the truth!

GABE. I wasn't home every night, like a good father?

STUART. You have no problem doing Michael's Bar Mitzvah in a cemetery,

GABE. Every night we ate supper together!

STUART. But for my Bar Mitzvah what did you do?

GABE. Six o'clock sharp. Every night, six o'clock!

STUART. What did you do?

GABE. What did I do?! What did I do?!

STUART. You don't remember?

GABE. Don't play games with me Stuart. What is it you want to say?

DIANE. Why did you boycott Stuart's Bar Mitzvah?

MICHAEL. What?!

GABE. You… told… her…?

STUART. She's my wife.

GABE. But Stuart, we had a pact. You, me, and Momme, we had a pact. We don't talk about this to strangers.

DIANE. I'm a stranger? I'm not a part of this family?

GABE. No, Mamele, I'm sorry but you're a visitor! You think you become a Jew by making Shabbes, say a few prayers, marry a Jew…instant Jew! You will never know what it is to be a Jew! Not an American Jew, but a European Jew! A Russian Jew! A German Jew! That's the Jew you will never know!

DIANE. I don't pretend to know Gabe. I'm just doing the best I can for my family and I didn't marry Stuart because he was Jewish. I married him because I love him and I converted because I wanted to. They were my choices Gabe. What choice did you make when you abandoned your son?

GABE. Leave me alone.

DIANE. Why weren't you there for him?

GABE. I said leave me –

DIANE. Why?

GABE. Don't give me your psychological drek!

DIANE. Why?

GABE. I'm not your patient!

MICHAEL. Zaydee, what happened?

GABE. *(beat)* I didn't go to your poppa's Bar Mitzvah.

MICHAEL. Why?

GABE. I was angry with God.

MICHAEL. But what did that have to do with Dad? God didn't kill the Jews, the Nazis did. That's what you say Zaydee, so why-

GABE. I told his Momma I would have no part of it!

DIANE. It wasn't yours, Gabe.

GABE. He had his Bar Mitzvah, I just wasn't there!

STUART. Why not Pop?

GABE. Oh Stuart it was thirty years ago! Move on.

STUART. Thirty years is a day.

GABE. *(appealing to the heavens)* R' boyn'e'sha-loy-lom!! What does he want from me?

STUART. Rabbi kept calling you up for your first Aleeyah… "Gavriel Ben Aryeh, Gavriel Ben Aryeh… Vu bistu" Vu bistu" Where are you? Where were you, Pop?

GABE. I couldn't go…

STUART. Everyone else came. Where were you? The synagogue was packed!

GABE. Packed with hypocrites!

STUART. Maybe so, but they came… for me. It was my day, and you missed it, missed my Haftarah, my speech, best speech of my life… I wrote it for you…

GABE. Stuart, I tried to come to Shul, but I was afraid I would spoil it for you. I would have raged against God.

STUART. I would have raged with you,

GABE. What did you know, you were a child.

STUART. I knew you weren't there. First I thought you were sick or got into an accident, or, died.

GABE. I was sick Stuart, sick with grief and hatred.

STUART. So, why didn't you tell me? Why didn't you talk to me?

GABE. About what, my nightmares?

STUART. Just talk to me.

GABE. Talk…

STUART. You never talked to me…

GABE. I wasn't a talking father! Talk! In America, everyone talks! It's a disease! There are some things you can talk from here till tomorrow, it wouldn't help! Some things you don't talk about!

STUART. I used to hear you scream at night… Momme would rock you till you fell back asleep. I'd stay up trying to think of ways to make you happy. Cause in my child's way of thinking, I believed that if I could make you happy, then everything would be okay and you could sleep. I couldn't wait for my Bar Mitzvah. I couldn't wait to chant my Haftarah for you, soothe you, make you proud of me, show you how much I loved you and wanted to be like you… I couldn't wait to have you stand beside me on the bima… feel your arm around me…two men chasing the demons away…

GABE. How childish to think a joyous occasion could make me happy. It only reminds me of what I lost.

STUART. Me too.

GABE. I make one mistake in thirty years!

STUART. One mistake?

GABE. I didn't come to your Bar Mitzvah, big deal!

MICHAEL. It is a big deal, Zaydee. What if your Poppa didn't come to your Bar Mitzvah?

GABE. So, he wouldn't come.

MICHAEL. You should have been there Zaydee.

GABE. Don't tell me what I should have done!

MICHAEL. All he wanted was your attention.

GABE. I gave him attention!

MICHAEL. Zaydee, you were his Poppa and you didn't go to his Bar Mitzvah.

GABE. So, we did other things!

STUART. Like?

GABE. *(pause)* So maybe I didn't do things with you, take you places, I didn't play with you. *(to EGON)* You, Schimdty, did your father play with you after the war?

EGON. My father died when I was seven.

GABE. Oh, ts, ts, ts, too bad.

EGON. Considering what you have been through Sir, could you have some decency?

STUART. I'm very sorry for my father,

GABE. Very nice a Jew apologizing to a Nazi.

STUART. That is uncalled for! *(with pace,* **GABE** *is relentless, goes after* **EGON***)*

GABE. Why you're not a Nazi?

STUART. That's enough!

GABE. You look like a Nazi, sound like a Nazi,

STUART. Did you hear me?!

GABE. Not to them, but to me!

STUART. I said that's enough!

GABE. So, you're not a Nazi?

EGON. No Sir, I am not!

GABE. And your father?

EGON. My father was a good man!

GABE. How about your grandfather?

STUART. How about the Ukrainians and Poles?

GABE. And your uncles?

STUART. Lithuanians and Czechs,

GABE. Uncles, father, grandfather,

STUART. American Jews who stood by and did nothing!

GABE. And their father –

STUART. Nothing!

GABE. And their father, and their father,

STUART. How far back do you want to go?

GABE. And their father and their father,

STUART. How far back?

DIANE. Stuart! Gabe! Stop!

STUART. Blame everyone!

DIANE. Stuart!

STUART. Carte Blanche blame!

GABE. *(goes after* **EGON***, taunting)* Do you know what they did?!

EGON. Sir!

DIANE. Gabe!

MICHAEL. Zaydee!

GABE. Do you?

MICHAEL. Leave him alone!

GABE. Do you?

EGON. Sir,

MICHAEL. He's only doing his job!

DIANE. Sit down, Michael!

GABE. Do you know what they did?

EGON. SIR!

GABE. DO YOU?!

EGON. SIR!

GABE. STOP CALLING ME SIR! My name is 3, 6, 7, 0, 7!

EGON. *(beat)* I will not call you by a number.

GABE. Why, you forgot how to count after six million? How do you people live with yourselves?

EGON. As best we can, Sir.

GABE. How do you think I live?

EGON. As best as you can, Sir.

GABE. Explain what your people did.

EGON. I cannot.

GABE. You hate us.

EGON. What happened is deeper than hate.

GABE. So, you have remorse? You have shame.

EGON. Of course, how can we not?

GABE. Shame of regret, or shame of failure?

EGON. Shame of loss!

GABE. Your only shame is, you lost the war. And we Jews won't let you forget it. We're a chicken bone stuck in your throat which you wish to cough up in Bitburg!

EGON. We're coughing up plenty, Sir, it's called reparations.

GABE. You can choke on your reparations, you think I like taking your money?!

EGON. No Sir, but you take it.

GABE. I would gladly give it all back when you give me my life back.

EGON. I cannot give you your life back, any more than you can give Germany back its self-respect.

GABE. Self-respect. You took our lives, burned our homes, our books, stole our art, our money, and now you're returning that money, so actually we're paying ourselves off! Except we're – Six-Million-Short!

EGON. I have nothing to do with the past! I repeat! I am innocent of your past!

GABE. You have nothing to do with your past, and he wants nothing to do with his. So, where does that leave me?

EGON. I don't know Sir. I can only be responsible for myself and I will not allow you to accuse me for crimes I did not commit!

GABE. The sins of your fathers are your sins!

EGON. I reject that.

GABE. You are all guilty!

EGON. I reject that!

GABE. All of you!

EGON. I reject that!

GABE. Reject all you want Schmidty. German Jews rejected their Judaism. They were still dragged off screaming, "I'm not a Jew! I'm not a Jew! What will you scream, "I'm not German! I'm not German?!"

EGON. I am German Sir. A good, proud German, and though I don't speak for all Germans as you sir certainly do not speak for all Jews, I am paying for the deeds of my fathers. They are not my deeds sir. But I am paying for them. So will my children, my grandchildren, and their children. Ten years in a thousand of Goethe, Beethoven, Heine, Rilke, Freud, Einstein, and all we'll be remembered for is murder! Innocent generations contaminated for eternity. Is that sufficient reparations for you Herr Stern?

GABE. I wouldn't be so concerned, Egon. You'll forgive yourselves long before we do.

EGON. For my children's sake, I hope so, Sir.

GABE. You have children?

EGON. Yes, sir

GABE. How many?

EGON. Two.

GABE. Boy, girl?

EGON. A boy and a girl.

GABE. How old is the boy?

EGON. Four.

GABE. And the little girl?

EGON. Two.

GABE. And, how old are you, Egon?

EGON. Twenty-four.

GABE. *(beat)* You know where I was at twenty-four?

EGON. The camps.

GABE. Dachau. You know Dachau?

EGON. I know of Dachau.

GABE. It's a tourist attraction now, with pretty gardens all around…Oh, if only the trees could speak… Several years ago, I returned to Dachau as part of a Gathering. It's a party for survivors. Every year we meet to remember, as if one could forget. Anyway, I was walking along, to where the crematorium once stood, and noticed a sign on the gate. A "NO SMOKING" sign.

EGON. The intention is to keep the area clean.

GABE. I know the intention. *(beat)* Michael, did I ever tell you how I ended up in Dachau?

MICHAEL. No.

GABE. Want to hear it?

MICHAEL. No!

GABE. It's a good story… Anyone else want to hear my story…my Dachau story…? *(All are silent.)* I was beaten, I was beaten by the Nazis when they marched into my little town. Do you know why I was beaten?

EGON. Because you are a Jew.

GABE. And because I wasn't a good truck washer. You see, the Nazis put me to work washing your dirty trucks and at the end of the day, the Nazi officer in charge put on a clean white glove and ran his finger along the side of the truck and then asked me why the white glove was dirty…and I said, because YOU ARE! Not the best thing to tell a Nazi. He hit me with his rifle, stuffed the glove in my mouth, and left me for dead. A friend carried me home, and when I recovered, my mother and sister Rochel, begged me to escape, to run away before I was killed… I didn't want to go. I really didn't want to go, because I knew, that if I left I would never see them again…but I left. I hid during the day and crawled at night. On the third day, I knocked on a farmer's door. The farmer was a good friend of my father. He used to sell us milk with eggs. The farmer and his wife took me in, gave me food, a blanket, hid me in the barn to sleep. I slept through the day and night. And when I woke…I was staring into the barrels of many rifles. And, as they dragged me off, the farmer, his wife, and his two little girls waved bye-bye. And that's how I came to Dachau…isn't that a good story? I didn't disappoint you, did I?

EGON. Sir, I am sorry for what happened to you.

GABE. More sorry than the farmer? …You know Egon, they say German farmers killed more Jews than did all the gas chambers. What do you think, Egon?

EGON. That's not a question is it?

GABE. No.

EGON. And you're not really interested in anything I have to say.

GABE. No.

EGON. Then may I ask you some questions?

GABE. Ask,

EGON. What is your regret?

GABE. That I left my mother and sister.

EGON. Yes, but what is your regret as a people?

GABE. What?

EGON. What is your shame as a people?

GABE. Our shame?

EGON. Don't you have shame? Collective shame?

GABE. For what, surviving?

EGON. For allowing yourselves to be slaughtered wholesale.

GABE. It was not our choice!

EGON. But, you did not resist.

GABE. Resist?! Do you think Dachau was a Hollywood movie? Dachau was towers and dogs and electric fences holding in fifty pound prisoners!

EGON. Yes, but before the camps, before the exterminations, during the round-ups, all over Europe, why did so many go so willingly?

GABE. Shtarker! You would have done better?!

EGON. I am only asking.

GABE. We were in shock! Collective shock!

EGON. But, you knew where you were going?

GABE. We did not know!

EGON. You knew! We knew! The world knew!

GABE. The world turned its back!

EGON. But you knew!

GABE. We did not know! We did not know where we were going!

EGON. You were stuffed into cattle cars, where did you think you were going?

GABE. To work. "Arbeit Macht Frei"

EGON. Incomprehensible.

GABE. Isn't it?

EGON. Yes! How do a people walk silently to their deaths and then only a few years later create Israel? Surrounded by millions of enemies in an unforgiving desert you rise… How? How is it possible? Why then and not before? Were you not the same people? Did it have to take a Holocaust to wake up? Why didn't you resist? Why didn't you fight back?

GABE. We did fight back! Did you never hear of the Warsaw Ghetto uprising? The Partisans? There were pockets of resistance all over Europe!

EGON. Pockets? We needed to be stopped!

GABE. Why didn't you stop yourselves?!

EGON. We couldn't, the country was out of control.

GABE. No Egon, you were in full control!

EGON. Sir, we were led by a maniac, good Germans were afraid for their lives.

GABE. Which were worth more than ours…Where were your heroes, Egon?…Why didn't you resist? Why didn't you fight back? We're you in collective shock too?… You can't stand to look at yourselves, so you blame the Jew.

EGON. I do not blame, Sir.

GABE. It's our fault,

EGON. No.

GABE. We asked for it,

EGON. You did not,

GABE. Because we did not resist,

EGON. No Sir!

GABE. We were weak, so we deserved to die.

EGON. That is ridiculous!

GABE. So what is the reason you murdered us?

EGON. I don't know, Sir.

GABE. What do they teach you in your schools, what do they tell you in your homes?

EGON. We don't talk about it.

GABE. You don't talk about it. Victims don't talk, murderers don't talk, a code of silence. Then maybe it would all just go away.

EGON. All I ever heard growing up, was why doesn't the world leave us alone, why, after so many years, are we still so hated?

GABE. Because you are the world's evil child. To this day, you believe you are the victims.

EGON. We all lost Sir, have we no right to heal?

GABE. No! You have no conscience, you have no rights!

EGON. Sir, I live with this war every day.

GABE. But you did nothing wrong.

EGON. You don't have to remind me of my innocence, Sir! Just stop hating me for what I did not do!

GABE. I should forgive you.

EGON. I have nothing to be forgiven for, but maybe you can forgive yourself.

GABE. Go to hell!

EGON. Sir, I am trying to understand what happened, but all you do is throw it back in my face! I I want to know the truth.

GABE. You don't know the truth.

EGON. Not from a survivor.

GABE. Stuart, can you help this man, he wants to know what happened.

STUART. I don't know what happened Pop, I just want to get the hell out of here!

GABE. Six million died and no one knows what happened. *(to* **EGON***)* Why don't you ask your father?! *(mashes a flower with his foot)*

EGON. Herr Stern, if you could kill every German responsible, would it lessen your hate any?

GABE. No.

EGON. Would it bring anyone back?

GABE. No.

EGON. Is it your wish for Michael to hate my children?

GABE. Yes.

EGON. How long must we wait Sir? *(overlapping)*

GABE. I will never forgive you!

EGON. Another forty, hundred, five hundred years?

GABE. Never!

EGON. Why don't we start here, now!

GABE. NO!

EGON. So what is your faith all about? Remembering to hate?

GABE. I don't remember to hate! I remember! *(pulls the shawl around him in prayer)*

EGON. Remember what? You wrap yourself in your prayer shawl to hate?

*(**GABE** is rocking back and forth in prayer. **EGON**, picks up a piece of the ripped protest sign puts it in **GABE**'s face.)*

Does this honor your people's sacrifice Sir?…Is this how you wish to be remembered?…Why don't you listen to me?

GABE. I don't trust you! I don't trust any German!

EGON. *(beat)* My grandfather did not trust Jews…an ordinary man, he owned a bicycle shop. Down the road, was another bicycle shop, more successful, owned by a Jew. Kristallnacht, my grandfather took his friends to the man's shop and burned it down with his wife and children inside. He hated just like you hate!

GABE. Don't confuse me with your grandfather!

EGON. My question is, when does it stop?

GABE. Never! You should all die! (*spits at his feet, steps on the flowers around the graves*)

P. A. ANNOUNCEMENT. (*voiceover*) VERLASSEN SIE DIEZEN PLATZ! (*Repeats*)

EGON. (*to* **STUART**) Remove your father, immediately! (**EGON** *on walkie talkie*)

DIANE. (*to* **GABE**) What's wrong with you?

GABE. He gives me confessions!

DIANE. He did nothing to you!

GABE. His grandfather murdered Jews! Burned them alive! And they get flowers? Why do they get flowers and we get ashes?!

DIANE. You want flowers? (*brings* **MICHAEL** *over*) Here's your flower! Look at him! This is your flower! This is what you should be fighting for!

GABE. Get away from me! (*pacing up and down*)

DIANE. I'm not saying forgive or forget! Just stop trying to make sense of it all. It's all so senseless, whose right, whose wrong, I'm right, you're right, Stuart's right, Egon's right, all of us are right, and in the end, we all lose.

P. A. ANNOUNCEMENT. (*voiceover*) VERLASSEN SIE DIEZEN PLATZ!

STUART. Let's go.

GABE. No!

STUART. They'll drag you out of here!

GABE. I must have courage! I must stay!

DIANE. Gabe, we have a life to get back to,

GABE. No life!

DIANE. Michael's Bar Mitzvah,

GABE. No, no,

MICHAEL. My Bar Mitzvah, Zaydee!

GABE. SHVEIG!!… (*breaks down*) What right do I have to live, when so many died?

STUART. Pop, you can't keep asking yourself that question. In ten, twenty years, all the guilty and all the innocent will have died…you have try to find some peace…

GABE. Peace…Where do I find peace?

DIANE. In your family, in our love for you.

STUART. In my love for you.

GABE. He never lived to tell me that…she never lived.

STUART. Who, Pop?

GABE. Oy kinder, a shtein, a stone sits in my heart,

DIANE. What stone?

GABE. Malke, n' Meechel, my wife and son,

STUART. *(stunned)* You had another family? Before Momme, before me?

GABE. I left them…

MICHAEL. Meechle… Michael.

STUART. I had a brother?

GABE. *(holds up two fingers)* Tzvei yor alt…

STUART. All these years, this wall between us…

GABE. Stuart, how could I go to your Bar Mitzvah when I would never live to see his? I curse the day I left!

MICHAEL. But the Nazi's would have killed you, Zaydee,

GABE. I should have stayed–

MICHAEL. Momme and Rochel begged you to escape.

GABE. Died with them.

MICHAEL. And then the farmer who turned you in,

GABE. There was no farmer! Michael, I did the most unforgivable thing a man can do, I left my family to save my own life.

MICHAEL. I don't understand.

GABE. That Nazi who beat me, he heard I was still alive and came to kill me, I saw him coming from my window, I was afraid, I ran into the woods…when I returned that night, they were gone…

EGON. *(into Walkie Talkie)* Vartin zie bitte.

GABE. After the war I searched every camp, asked every lantzman...did you happen to see my wife, my family, my baby...would you know where they went? No one knew. No one saw. But I saw. Every night I saw their faces,...the faces I look for in the stones I chisel...How Stuart? How do you live again when everything you loved, everything you lived for is destroyed and you remain the witness?

STUART. I don't know, pop, how could I know?

GABE. Momme used to say, "Gabe, we must live. We must mourn and we must live." I could only mourn...

STUART. And yet you gave to Michael...

GABE. I couldn't do it with you Stuart. I would come home from work, I'd stand outside the door and talk to myself..."Gabe, Gabe,... don't bring your misery into the house...be kind, be gentle, play with your son, read him a book, sing him a song... simple things. The simple things a father does to show his love... I couldn't do. *(viciously towards* EGON*)* Because of him and his people, I lost a life and you lost a childhood!

EGON. Is there anything else you wish to blame me for, Sir? There are evil people in this world, but I am not one of them. I am sorry for what happened, I am ashamed of what my people did, there are not enough apologies. Apologies cannot replace what you lost. Nothing can. But it seems Sir, you wish to remain broken, I do not. The sins of my father's are not my sins, they are only my responsibility, my burden, I carry them, I accept them, but you Sir do not accept me... you ask your son to forgive you.

(GABE *looks at* STUART *slumped on the bench, head down.*)

He should understand what you went through. But do you understand him? Do you understand me? It is hard enough, but when the innocent cannot forgive themselves...too often the wrong people die, Herr Stern. You regret not being a better father? I had no father. My father died a young man, consumed by his father's crime. *(removes a medal in a handkerchief from his pocket)* During Israel's war in 1967, my father volunteered. He was a doctor, and one night, a rocket hit the hospital. So, here I am with this medal of service to remember him by. *(places the medal in **GABE***'s hand)* But, what do I do Sir? Where do I go? Where do I seek my reparations if not in your heart? Am I not a son too?

GABE. Yes, Egon, you are a son, too.

EGON. *(pause)* Sir,…would you come to my home? I don't live far from here, and you could meet my wife and children…*(**GABE** doesn't move.)*

MICHAEL. He's trying to be your friend, Zaydee…don't be stubborn, if Bubbe Molly were here, she'd say "don't be stubborn Gabe," and you would listen. She'd say, "Gabe, be a Mentsch,"…be kind, be gentle, be a human being…isn't that what you tell me? Be a Mentsch? *(**GABE** is silent.)* I don't know what else to say Zaydee… I know its hard for you, and I wish I could make it easier and I thought I did when I came here and you told me I gave you hope…that's what a man does, right?… He gives someone hope…can you help me do that for you, Zaydee?…I'm your Boytschick.

EGON. Come to my home… I will serve you…

GABE. *(beat)* Of all the millions of Germans, they send me the one clean one.

EGON. I am not alone sir.

GABE. You'll forgive me, Egon, but I can't be a guest in your home, but I will walk with you. It's time for both of us to leave this sad place…

*(**GABE** stands, turns, and stops to look at his son sitting alone. On the way over to **STUART**, **GABE** is kissed on the cheek by **DIANE**. **GABE** then removes his own Talis, drapes it around **STUART**'s shoulders, and signals for **MICHAEL**'s yarmulke, placing it on **STUART**'s head. **STUART** stands, they look looks at each other*

and embrace. As they come out of the embrace, exiting, **STUART** *begins chanting his Haftarah.* **GABE** *puts his arm around* **STUART** *'s shoulder. Military music filters in, lights fade as they leave Bitburg cemetery, arms around each other, followed by* **DIANE** *and* **MICHAEL**, **EGON**, *who takes one look back.)*

End of Play